Angel:
A Hustling Diva with a Twist
By Brenda G. Wright

To order additional copies of this book, contact:
Xlibris Corporation
1-888-795-4274
www.Xlibris.com
Orders@Xlibris.com
111450

Table of Contents

Chapter One
The Beginning of Angel:
A Hustling Diva-Turned-Assassin

ANGEL WAS BORN and raised in the Lower West Side of Chicago; she was born to Gloria Black, a crackhead. Gloria, nicknamed "Glow," was the neighborhood slut; she had sex with every man in the hood, trying to keep her habit going.

Gloria met this guy one day going into a crack house. Glow was a pretty black woman with a caramel complexion with long silky black hair; she weighed one hundred and thirty pounds and stood five feet six.

This guy looked and saw potential in Glow; he took an immediate interest in her look. She was a crackhead, but she kept her appearance up. Everyone in the hood knew what Glow was about, and they also knew the Hawaiian kingpin Cane. Cane was a mobster; he ran the West Side and South Side, and he had a whole army of soldiers under his wing.

Cane didn't take no shorts when it comes to his money; Cane was a very handsome man with dark skin, slender-built; he had a swagger worse than Denzel; he dressed the part of his kingpin status, and he also owned a club called Club Sexy that had strippers dancing on poles and a gambling room in the back.

Cane also had a dope room on the second floor. The man didn't sell ounces; he was the heavyweight. If you wanted to purchase some weight, Cane was the man; Cane couldn't get the image out of his mind of this beautiful crackhead female he had seen two days ago. He wanted to go back in the hood just to see if she was still there, but he decided against it because he didn't roll like that.

Cane came up with the idea to send his right-hand man to the crack house he owned to see if Glow was hanging out there, and to his dismay, she was there

1

and had been there all night. He didn't want her to know at the time he had his soldiers watching out for her.

It was something about her that kept his mind on lock. He couldn't shake the feeling she had on him; no female had ever had that kind of power over the kingpin Cane. Cane knew he had to investigate her to find out who she was and how she got into that predicament.

Cane knew she was going to be his as soon as he could pinpoint her problems. One day, he received a call stating that Glow was at the crack house having a seizure, and they were getting ready to call an ambulance. He told the caller not to call the ambulance and that he would send someone to pick her up and bring her to him. He told the caller to make sure she didn't bite her tongue and to keep her comfortable until her ride gets there.

When Cane's right-hand man got there to pick Glow up, she was unconscious. The sight of her made Cane to sweat, and he deeply admired her beauty; he wanted nothing more but for her to be healthy and safe. The next morning, when Glow came to she didn't know where she was or why she was in a place she didn't recognize.

She realized she was in a place that was so beautiful that she knew this had to be a dream. She saw houses like that only in magazines; she did recognize the handsome man in front of her, but what she didn't understand was why her. She soon found out that she held the key to Cane the kingpin's heart.

Cane kept her in a room with a doctor to help her kick her cocaine habit; it was the longest two weeks of her life. When she had finally kicked her habit, she knew Cane wanted something in return.

Cane had his maid to fix breakfast for Glow, and when she was done eating breakfast, he asked if she would like to meet him out on his terrace, and she did. Then he told Glow that he didn't want anything in return, but he just wanted to be her man if she would have him.

Glow remembered how she grew up poor and how she got molested all the time by her mother's boyfriends and close relatives in her father's family. So what else could she possibly lose? She decided right then and there that if he wanted to have a place in her life, then she wanted everything that money could buy.

Glow became queen bee of all of Cane's crack houses, and Club Sexy became her number one spot. Cane took Glow on shopping trips to New York, Las Vegas, and Paris, France. She spent money like she was born wealthy. Cane was happy to spoil Glow; she meant the world to him, and he knew one day she would rule his castle.

Cane wanted Glow to shine, so he took her to Tiffany's. Cane iced out

Glow's body with white diamonds from head to toe. Cane wanted to have a party to reintroduce her to the people in the hood who knew her as Glow the Crackhead; she was draped in a five-thousand-dollar Donna Karan dress and three-thousand-dollar Donna Karan stilettos and the bag to match.

When she stepped out of her dressing room, she was in a cloud; her man Cane had on a royal blue Donna Karan suit to match her dress. Cane had on some royal blue Donna Karan snakeskin banisters. They both were a force to reckon with. Cane went all out for the woman he's going to ask to be his wife.

Cane and Glow had been going hot and heavy for two years now; they even bought a house with five bedrooms and five bathrooms and three car garage for the three cars: Rolls-Royce, Jaguar, and a Hummer. The kitchen was set up with all stainless steel appliances; the house was decorated with beautiful marble floors.

The furniture was designed by Donna Karan; also she decorated each room with precise detail. Cane made sure the house was picture-book-perfect; the house was named number one in the weekly magazine.

Cane and Glow have been going hot and heavy in the sex department. Glow even missed her period for three months; she didn't even notice she was being so happy until one morning they were having breakfast, and Cane looked at her rear end and noticed she had more junk in her trunk and they laughed.

Glow didn't do like most women; she didn't have morning sickness at all, but her breast and butt picked up a little weight. Glow decided that morning after breakfast she would go pay the doctor office a visit as a walk-in because she couldn't wait; she wanted to know as soon as possible. Glow finished her breakfast, took a quick shower, and headed out for the doctor's office.

She did the usual tests, and to her surprise, she was three months pregnant. She was scared and happy at the same time, not because she was with a baby but it scared her that because she was pregnant by a Hawaiian kingpin that will kill at the drop of a hat.

Glow knew in her heart that Cane loved her, and their child would have everything that she or he wanted. When Glow finally made it home from the doctor's office, Cane was sitting in his office, waiting to hear the good news; he knew he didn't shoot blanks.

Cane also knew that he had to make dinner arrangements for his marriage proposal. Cane had to make sure everything was right. The ring that he purchased for Glow was a twenty-thousand-dollar ten-carat pink platinum diamond engagement ring. Cane had the Terrace decked out like they were in Hawaii; the palm trees were beautiful and the dinner menu was off the chain.

The chef prepared lobster, crab salad, steamed vegetables, and buttered bread sticks; for dessert, they had chocolate mousse; the music that was playing softly in the background was one of Teddy Pendergrass songs: "Turn off the Lights." She didn't even think a man of his caliber had it going on like that.

The lights were dimmed, and he took her hand into his and gazed into her eyes, and he asked her would she be his wife and she said yes without a second thought; she wanted to marry this man. She fell in love with him in six months' time. She didn't even know his real government name and that's when it hit Glow to ask. As she was about to ask him, he reached his hand out to introduce himself to her as Clarence Cantrell Carter a.k.a. Cane. Six months later, their little bundle of joy was born: seven pounds and six ounces. She was born with curly black hair and big hazel brown eyes. She was the most beautiful baby Glow had ever seen. Clarence and Gloria Carter agreed to name their newborn as Angel Candice Carter a.k.a. Baby Girl—the beginning of the hustling diva with a twist.

After Angel was born, Cane started taking long trips to California for business meetings without Glow; she never questioned what he was doing out of town because she knew and trusted her man until one day, in particular, when Cane came home all of a sudden. The phone would ring, and when she answered, the caller on the other end would hang up. Glow just chopped it up as someone playing on the phone.

Cane went straight into his daughter's room; he loved watching her sleep; he knew his Baby Girl was as beautiful as her mother; Cane had made plans to take his beautiful wife out for dinner that night to tell her he had plans on going on another business trip; this time he will be gone for two weeks.

He didn't know how she would handle it, so he had to push the right buttons because he learned one thing about Glow that she didn't play when it comes to her man. When he told Glow what his plans were, she felt a bad feeling in her stomach, so she asked Cane was he taking any of his soldiers with him. He told her no and could handle his business on his own. Since the situation didn't sit right with Glow, she had to trust her man.

Two days later, Cane was packing for his two-week trip, and Glow still harvested the same funny feelings she had the night Cane told her about his trip. She didn't say anything because she wasn't about to spoil her man's trip.

She started getting those anonymous phone calls again with the phone ringing all times of night with no one on the other end, so she would take the phone off the hook at night so she could get a peaceful night's sleep while her Baby Girl was asleep.

Cane would call her every night at seven, so she felt safe taking the phone off the hook at night after the call. One night, she was awakened out of her sleep by a dream she was having about Cane: he was in trouble. She could feel the pain he was in, and it frightened her so bad she broke out in a sweat.

Glow put the phone back on the hook to give Cane a call, and when she called his hotel room, she didn't get an answer, which really frightened her, so she called the hotel's front desk, and to her dismay, Cane didn't even have a room at the hotel he told her he was going to be staying in, which really made Glow get out of bed and make some calls to Cane's soldiers and right-hand man.

She knew if anyone knew what was going on, it is his right-hand man, Silk. Glow called Silk, and he answered on the first ring. She asked Silk had he heard anything from Cane; he told her that he had spoken to Cane that morning and everything was all right with him.

Glow didn't believe Silk because her feelings were telling her something different, so she decided she had to do a little investigation on her own, but before she could get dressed, the doorbell rung and the ups man was standing there with a box waiting for her signature.

When she opened up the box, she screamed out loud and almost passed out. Inside the box was the head of Cane, the Hawaiian kingpin. She cried so loud until she woke up their Baby Girl.

She had to pull herself together and call Silk so he could tell her what the hell was going on and who was Cane involved with that they wanted his head on a silver platter. Glow was concerned because she couldn't have a proper funeral for Cane without a body.

Glow decided to have a marmoreal for Cane, but she wasn't giving up on him; someone had to tell her what happened to her husband. Silk, the right-hand man, always had a secret crush on Glow, but he wasn't about to cross Cane while he was still alive anyway.

Glow couldn't pull herself together without Cane; he saved Glow from a life of destruction, pain, and suffering. Glow didn't think she could be on her own without the man who pulled her out of the gutter.

Silk knew she needed Cane, and he knew without him he could slide in and make things better for Glow, but what Silk didn't know was that Glow felt like he was a suspect in what happened to Cane. Glow was never going to trust him. What Glow didn't know was Cane left her wealthy for the rest of her life, and Silk knew of this. That's why he had a part in what happened to Cane with the Italian mafia.

Chapter Two
Cane's Double Life

CANE WAS LIVING a double life that Glow knew nothing about. When Cane met Glow, he was already married to a black woman of Italian origin named Rakia Salvador; her father was the head of the Italian mafia. Cane worked for him. That's how Cane came up in life. He had nothing when he met Rakia.

He moved to Chicago to take over one of the family business but didn't know he was being watched the whole time. Cane and Rakia had two sons together that were being trained to join the family business on their twenty first birthdays.

Cane's father-in-law's right-hand man Don sent Mr. Salvador information on Cane and Glow's wedding and birth of their daughter. The news made Mr. Salvador very angry, and that how Cane could treat Rakia like trash didn't sit well with him; Cane had to pay for his mistakes. He called Cane on his private phone and demanded that he come spend some time with the family.

Cane did what he was ordered to do because he knew what Mr. Salvador was about. He knew he didn't want to take any chances knowing he had another family he had to protect. Cane arrived in Hawaii as planned. He was there three days before the shit hit the fan.

They were all having dinner when Mr. Salvador wanted to discuss some family business with Cane, so they went to Mr. Salvador's office with four of his bodyguards following close behind like they always did. Mr. Salvador reached in his cigar box to get a cigar; he lit it and took a long drag.

Mr. Salvador reached across his desk for an envelope that was delivered to him by one of his right-hand men, and when he opened it up and shoved them to Cane, his face turned blue. He knew he was in very dangerous waters. He couldn't believe that his father-in-law was having him followed.

Mr. Salvador looked at Cane and asked him one question: how long did you think that I was going to let you drag my family through the mud? Cane had a look on his face that made Mr. Salvador to shiver because Cane knew what was going to happen to him. Cane just wasn't ready to leave Glow and their Baby Girl behind; pictures of them flashed before his eyes. Only thing he could do was say good-bye in his mind.

Mr. Salvador told one of his bodyguards to tie Cane up; then they dragged him down in the cellar, where they tortured him for five days straight. Mr. Salvador wanted Cane to feel the pain that he put his daughter through with his two young sons watching. Cane's pain wasn't going to be emotional but was going to be physical.

Cane knew Mr. Salvador had a couple of pit bulls around on the grounds but never in a thousand years Cane would have thought that he would become the pit bulls meal of the day.

Mr. Salvador hired a hooker to get Cane on hard for the pit bulls. The bodyguards had all ready stripped him of all his clothing. When the hooker was done performing her job, Cane was up and running. The bodyguards gave the hooker hamburger meat to wrap around Cane's penis.

The hooker did as she was told and was dismissed by one of the bodyguards never to remember what she saw. One of the bodyguards wrapped a chain around Cane's neck; what they did next was unbelievable. The bodyguard, they called Killer, was mad crazy; Killer took Cane's eyeballs out, put red pepper on them, and fed them to the pit bulls.

Cane was swinging from a beam in the middle of the floor while the bodyguards beat him until he passed out. They thought that Cane was dead because he lost so much blood. Killer and his crew were sitting around when they heard a sound come from Cane; the pit bulls were there. Also the next thing they did was to wrap the hamburger meat back around Cane's penis for the dogs to eat, and the pit bulls chewed on Cane's penis until he passed out again.

When Cane came to consciousness again, the chain around his neck was so tight that he was choking off his own blood. The bodyguards started twisting his body around until his head popped off and blood shot everywhere, and Mr. Salvador had them to get rid of the body and box the head up and ship it to his new wife as a warning never to mess with the Salvador family.

But before the box got delivered to Glow, the box was intercepted at ups by Silk, Cane's right-hand man. He didn't want Glow to find out about Cane's secret life before he had a chance to clear his name from the book of suspects. It wasn't long before Glow started fading into some of her bad habits again; Silk knew he had to gain her trust so he could get his hands on some of that fortune Cane left behind.

What Silk didn't know was Cane's Baby Girl was going to be groomed to take over her father's empire; she was growing up pretty fast. Cane was dead and gone now for a year, and Baby Girl was growing up like a tweed.

One day, Silk came over to talk with Glow, and she was so distraught over Cane she never was the same Glow: started drinking like crazy, letting her appearance go down, and her weight fell off; she had to pull herself together for Baby Girl.

Glow left the living room, where she and Silk were talking, to answer her phone. While she was out of the room, Silk spiced her drink; that was his way of getting Glow on track of her set back. Little did Silk know that Glow had cameras set up in every room of her house. So she watched every move that Silk made.

When Glow entered her living room area, Silk was sitting there with a half-smile on his face. She wanted to turn that smile of his upside down, but she knew that wasn't the right time or place, but she did have big plans for Mr. Silk.

One night, Glow was asleep in her bedroom when a vision of Cane appeared in the bedroom doorway; he looked as good to her the day he left for his two-week trip, but something about the vision threw her off: he looked worried, and his skin didn't have that glow that she was used to seeing.

Cane lead Glow over to the center of the room where he had a floor safe, and he put his fingers up so he could give her the combination to the safe. She couldn't believe what she was seeing because he never told her about the safe before.

When Glow unlocked the safe, she was devastated. There were documents of the Hawaiian crime family that she could bury them with, plus it was incriminating evidence about his business as well. What she really found out next in those documents is that Silk, Cane's right-hand man, was Cane's son from another crackhead he met before he hooked up with the mafia family.

Silk didn't know Cane was his father because Cane had his mother killed because she threatened to tell the mafia family and his wife Rakia about their bastard son. Cane couldn't have that, so the only way he would be sure that wouldn't happen was to make sure Silk's mother had a permanent dirt nap.

Glow also found documents that would leave Baby Girl set for life as well. Glow had pictures of everyone in the mafia family, so she knew that Cane left all that information there for her to protect herself and their daughter. Cane also left a map of a safe house if she ever needed to go there.

Cane explained in a letter that he wrote Glow about his bad choices and mishaps with the life he was living. He even told her his father was a pimp and his mother was a crackhead who sold him out to the highest bidder.

Cane told Glow in the letter that if it weren't for this old man in the Hawaiian village where he was born, he wouldn't even know her the old man saved his life. Cane also told Glow that Silk was not to be trusted, and to protect their daughter with all cost, Glow spent the night looking over all the information she had in her hand and decided it was time to put a plan together for her daughter just in case something happened to her. She wanted to make sure Baby Girl had the same information Cane had given to her.

Two days went by and Glow hadn't heard anything from Silk, which made Glow a little uneasy. So she made a few calls to see where Silk was, only if she knew Silk stayed, camped outside Glow's house, a few houses down in an unmarked car, keeping his eyes on his fortune.

Silk had his mind wondering with thoughts of how he could come up with another master plan that's not so obvious to Glow. Deep in Silk's heart, he knew Glow was on to him. All of a sudden, he had a premonition that he could get on Glow's good side and set her up with a drug bust. Silk wasn't trying to take Glow completely out of the picture. He just wanted what was due to him.

He thought that since he set Cane up and now that Cane was dead, he deserved Cane's empire. Silk decided to stay invisible for a while. He wanted Glow to come to him; he didn't want to seem too desperate. Silk didn't know that Glow was going to do just that she had plans for Silk's demise herself.

Silk was mostly in hiding because he was on the phone one day talking to one of Mr. Salvador's bodyguards, and one of Cane's foot soldiers heard his conversation on the setup of Cane's demise.

Silk didn't know what the foot soldier heard, but he knew it was enough to get him killed if Glow ever found out about it. What Silk didn't know was that Tony, Cane's foot soldier, was Cane's son too. Neither one of them knew that they were related to each other. Tony knew what he was hiding from Glow would either break her down or tear her apart.

Tony knew he had to do something quick because he was a loyal foot soldier to Cane, and Tony never trusted Silk; he knew he was trouble the first day Cane bought him on the set. Tony knew when he stepped to Glow with any kind of information, he had to have all his facts straight.

Tony waited another day before he gave Glow a call to ask if he could meet with her about some serious business he had to discuss with her. She hadn't heard from Tony in a while, so she agreed to meet with him to see what Tony had to talk about.

Glow asked Tony to meet her downtown at Club Sexy. He asked Glow what time, and she told Tony to be there at seven thirty, and he agreed. Glow was happy to see Tony because he was loyal to her and Cane. She knew she could trust Tony with her life.

Glow ordered her and Tony a drink of their choice, and the conversation started by Tony telling Glow how beautiful she was. He asked her how her daughter was doing. Glow said that her daughter was fine.

"I know you didn't call this meeting to ask me about my daughter, so what's really going on, Tony."

"Well, let me start by asking you have you heard from Silk lately."

"No. Have you?"

"No. But I know he set Cane up to be killed by the mafia family."

At first, Glow sat there staring at Tony. In her mind, she knew he had to know something because how would Tony know about the mafia if she didn't tell him unless Tony and Cane was much closer than she thought.

"Glow, are you all right because all the color just left out your face."

"Yes, Tony, I'm fine. Now stop bullshitting and get on with the story."

"I was supposed to be on the set that day Cane left to go on his two-week vacation, but I left late because when I got up that morning, I had the bubble guts.

"I thought I was in the house by myself, but I heard voices coming from Cane's office in the back. Everybody knows not to go in Cane's office and never touch his private phone line, so I stood by the door so I could hear who was in Cane's office. When I heard Silk's voice, I knew it was some shit going down, so I stood there very quiet to see what Cane's trusted right-hand man had to say. What I heard Silk say next blew me out the water. Silk was basically putting a hit out on the man he was supposed to protect with his life."

Tony knew Silk wasn't shit from the beginning, but who was going to believe him. Tony tried to confront Cane about Silk's evil ways on several occasions, but he wouldn't listen because Silk and Tony would always fight for the attention of Cane, if it wasn't over driving Cane around to picking which dope spot they ran for the day.

Glow was serious about the conversation Tony was having with her, so she started asking questions about what Tony knew about the Italian mafia. What Tony knew was devastating to Glow because what he said to her rung truth to her because it was the same stuff she read in the information Cane left for her in the safe.

What puzzled Glow the most was how could this man say he love me and live a double life. Glow felt stupid because how could she live with Cane and not know him at all. That day Tony and Glow decided to band together and handle their business with Silk.

Three days later, Silk decided he had to put his plan in motion; his plan was to steal two keys of dope from the dope house with three AK-47s to plant in

Glow's house. Silk had to find a way to get into Glow's house undetected because her house was armed like Fort Knox's.

Silk came up with the idea to cut the wires to the cameras and to the alarms systems. Once he did that, he knew getting in wouldn't be a problem. He knew to pick the day: Baby Girl would be at school so he didn't frighten her and Glow would be at Club Sexy.

Two days later, Glow got up from bed, fixed breakfast, and got Baby Girl ready for her to be dropped off at school, and Glow kept going until she reached Club Sexy. Glow went to Club Sexy twice a week to make sure everything was running smoothly. After Glow left Club Sexy, she felt a cold chill run down her spine; it made her break out in a sweat. Glow knew something wasn't right. It also felt like she was being followed.

Glow thought back to the day Cane and she were riding, and he thought he was being followed, so he pulled into a gas station. So Glow did the same thing just to see if her woman's intuition kicked in. When Glow pulled into the station, the car kept going, so Glow was cool with that, but her woman's intuition still wasn't sitting right with Glow.

Glow called Tony to see what was up with him, and he told Glow that he was being followed by someone driving a dark blue charger without any plates. Tony didn't know who it was, but he told Glow to be careful just in case because Silk was still in the city somewhere. Glow told Tony she would and for him to do the same, and they hung up without another word to each other.

Glow knew she and Tony were on the same page; something wasn't right. Glow went shopping at the mall when she hung up with Tony because Baby Girl needed some more new clothes. All the while Glow was in the shopping mall, Silk was buzzing around Glow's house trying to convince himself to cut off the cameras and alarm systems.

As Glow was at the counter paying for her daughter's clothes, something told her she needed to go home. Glow got in her charger, hit the freeway, and made it home just in time because Silk was just about to enter Glow's house through the back door when he heard the garage door sliding up.

Silk slid down to the ground and eased his way into the bushes. He made his way to the side of the house where Glow couldn't see him. Silk made his way back down the street where he had his unmarked car parked. Silk looked in his rearview mirror and said to himself, *Damn! I almost got busted. What if she checked the wires or something?*

Silk had to come up with a fireproof plan for real and escape route as well. Silk said to himself, *Back to the drawing board.* What silk didn't know was that Glow had a lady that lived across the street from her watching her house.

When Glow had the repairman to come and hook her cameras and alarm systems back up, Glow knew she had to get in contact with Tony so they can get their heads together to come up with a plan to take Silk off the map.

That night, Tony came over to Glow's house to discuss the plan Tony came up with: it was to lower Silk to a drug meeting being that Silk was all about the Benjamin's. Tony also knew he was taking a dangerous chance because Silk had been trying to find Tony every since he peeped him listening to his conversation with the mafia family.

Tony ran the scenario down to Glow on how the plan was going to work. She was happy to be a part of giving Silk a dirt nap. Tony told Glow this was going to be a real drug transaction, so they have to come up with at least fifty thousand dollars apiece.

Glow told Tony that will work. What Glow didn't know for sure was how it was going to play out. But to be on the safe side, Glow took one of the AK-47s and two extra clips; she wanted to be more safe than sorry.

When Tony called Silk and set up the meeting, he agreed to meet with him in one of Cane's secluded warehouses. Tony knew what Silk was talking about because it was nothing out there but dirt roads and trees. They had killed and chopped up so many people out there before when Cane was alive.

Silk put a call in to one of the other foot soldiers that used to work for Cane that he could trust the name Short Stack. Short Stack didn't like Tony because he thought Tony was a ass-kissing Uncle Tom, so when Silk called to let Short Stack know what's up, he was ready; he told Silk he had been waiting for an opportunity to put two in Tony's head.

While on the West Side of town, Tony and Glow were getting their firepower together so was Silk and Short Stack. Silk was running down to Short Stack about the situation with Glow, but he didn't tell him about the money at all, but he didn't have to. Everybody that was a part of Cane's drug business knew what was up.

Short Stack had a plan of his own as well. He called his twin brother Snake to come along with him to watch his back. As Short Stack was explaining the situation to his brother, the phone rang, and it was Silk, letting him know it was time to bounce.

Short Stack told his brother he will be at his house in ten minutes to get his guns and be outside. Glow and Tony were already at the warehouse waiting for Silk's arrival, not knowing Silk had backup as well. When Silk made it to the warehouse, he noticed Tony's car sitting there, so he told Short Stack to give him twenty minutes before he come in.

When Silk entered the warehouse, Tony stepped out from behind the lumber they had against the wall.

Silk said, "Where the money at, Tony?"

"I have the money. Where are the drugs?"

Tony knew something was about to go down because Silk kept reaching for his side. Before Tony could say anything else, Short Stack and Snake came in, blazing, hitting Silk and Tony, ripping Silk apart. Tony fell behind the lumber, and Glow came up with the AK-47, hitting Short Stack and Snake so fast they didn't even see it coming.

Glow helped Tony out of the warehouse before she left. She wanted to make sure Silk and his sidekicks are dead. After Glow got Tony to the car, she went back into the warehouse to make sure that she and Tony didn't leave any evidence of them ever being there. When Glow made it back to the car, Tony had passed out. She didn't know what to do. She remembered the doctor Cane went to about a gunshot wound, so she got him to come to her house to take care of Tony.

Tony had been shot three times: once in the chest and two times in the abdomen. Tony was losing blood fast, and Glow was scared Tony was going to die. By the time the doctor got there, Tony was still out cold, but the doctor did emergency surgery on Tony in Glow's garage, took the bullets out, and gave Glow pain pills for Tony, and the doctor left ten thousand dollars richer.

Glow felt good knowing she didn't have to watch her back no more because Silk was taking a dirt nap so she thought. She waited for the news to come on that night because she wanted to hear about the warehouse shooting, but it didn't air on the news for two days. The second day, it aired on TV when Glow was in the kitchen, fixing dinner for her and her daughter. When the breaking news came on reporting the warehouse shooting of two guys known as Short Stack and Snake, which was their street name, no one could identify their bodies because they where rip to shreds. Glow got worried then because the news only mentioned two guys—not three, so Glow knew she had to get Baby Girl somewhere safe.

Glow decided to take her daughter to the safe house that Cane had wrote her about. When she got there, she was shocked: the house was beautiful and the fridge was stocked full of food. Glow knew she couldn't be in hiding too long with her daughter because her child had to go to school. Glow didn't have any family in Chicago, so she had to think of something quick. She had to get her daughter out of town and somewhere safe.

Glow was sitting there thinking when a light came on in her head. She thought about her aunt Marie that stayed in Ohio. She was good with Glow when the state came in and took Glow after her mother got killed. Glow just didn't know how she was going to go and talk to her aunt. She hadn't seen her aunt Marie in years. She didn't even know if she was still alive, but she knew she had to try.

Glow went and got the white pages to see if she could find her aunt's address and phone number, and lo and behold, she found Aunt Marie. Glow gave Aunt Marie a call, and they talked for hours. She asked Glow to come and visit her soon. Little did she know Glow would be there to visit her sooner than she thought.

Two days later, Glow was on a plane, taking her Baby Girl to meet her aunt Marie. When she arrived, she got a rental car and drove to Aunt Marie's house and was happy to see Aunt Marie who was doing very well for herself. Aunt Marie heard a knock on her door. When she opened the door and saw Glow standing there with this beautiful little girl, it brought back memories of when the state department bought Glow to her house. Aunt Marie broke down crying with joy. She knew something wasn't right with Glow from the expression she had on her face.

After Aunt Marie fed them lunch, she asked Angel did she want to go and watch television while she talked to her mother. She looked at Glow and asked her what was going on with her because she knew for her to show up at her door after ten years something had to be wrong. Glow gave Aunt Marie her life history: every detail from her being a crackhead until the day she married the Hawaiian kingpin.

Glow even told her aunt about Cane's head being delivered to her house in a box. Glow left Aunt Marie with instructions if she didn't make it back to get her daughter She also left a bank account with her to take care of her Baby Girl. Aunt Marie told Glow she will take care of her daughter with her life, and she didn't have to worry about her as long as she was alive.

Glow spent the night, got up the next morning, and headed back to Chicago. She took the rental back and caught the next flight out to Chicago. When Glow arrived in Chicago, she had a funny feeling in her stomach. She felt like all eyes were on her; she knew that feeling all too well. She knew she had to find out Silk's whereabouts fast because she didn't want to keep watching her back. What Glow didn't know was Tony was on the case while she was in hiding: he had peeped Silk sitting down the street from Glow's house in an unmarked dark blue sedan.

Tony had already set a trap for Silk. He wanted Silk to suffer slowly for what he did to Cane. He was waiting on it to get dark so he could slip up behind him and rock him to sleep so he could take him somewhere secluded. Silk was sitting in his car down the street and waiting on Glow to return when he felt a sharp pain in his neck. Tony had snuck in Silk's car when he got out his car to take a piss.

Tony couldn't believe how lucky he was: he tied Silk up, took him to a vacant house, and waited on Glow to call. Four hours later, Glow was on her way to the vacant house. When Glow arrived at the house, Silk was wide awake from the heroin Tony had shot in his neck. Silk looked up and saw Glow and started pleading for his life because he knew Glow was about her business.

Glow asked Silk what did Cane do to him to make him set him up the way he did. What Silk said next shocked the shit out of Glow.

He told Glow, "That bastard killed my mother. Cane didn't even want me to know that I was his son. I found out I was his son by snooping around in his office one day. My birth certificate was in his safe. Dumbass fucker should have hid it better.

"Go ahead, bitch. Kill me. I ain't got shit. I'm better off dead anyway. But before you do, I want you to know Mr. Salvador knows about you and your daughter and he's going to kill both of y'all."

Glow got so upset with that statement. She slapped the shit out of Silk because he didn't know she knew about Mr. Salvador and his whole mafia family.

Tony said, "That's enough talking. It's time for Silk to meet his maker."

Tony had a big can of battery acid and poured it all over Silk's body. Slowly, he wanted to hear him scream out in pain. Tony started putting the acid on Silk's face first. It melted his skin off like hot grease at a fish fry.

After Tony had finished with Silk, it wasn't nothing left to clean up; Silk was history. Glow and Tony left the vacant house and never spoke of Silk again. They became close friends after the death of Silk.

Chapter Three
The Death of Gloria Carter a.k.a. Glow

GLOW STILL WASN'T sure about being out of danger just yet. She wanted to get some personal business in order before she went to Aunt Marie's to pick up her daughter, but Glow didn't think it was safe to go back home just yet. She started feeling lonely one night, sitting there looking at pictures of her and Cane.

She decided she needed some company to keep her on the right track. She didn't have any female friends. She only knew of one person she could call on and that was Tony, but she really didn't want to bother Tony, but she really did need to talk to someone. She picked up the phone to call Tony when she heard a knock at the door. She peeped out the keyhole to see Tony standing there with a bottle of Moët.

She said, "You must have been reading my mind. I was just going to give you a call to see what you were up to."

What Glow didn't know about Tony was he had his own agenda. He wanted to get a little closer to Glow as well. He wanted to know what made a kingpin like Cane marry a crackhead like Glow. Either she had some good head or she was good in between the sheets.

So Tony thought that if he could get her drunk, she might be willing to share. Tony wanted to become Glow's lover, but he knew he was probably too young. But he said to himself, *Nothing beats a failure, but a try what can it hurt.* Glow and Tony sat there all night getting toasted. When he looked up, Glow said she be right back she had to use the restroom.

When Glow came back into the room, she had on a long silk gown with nothing on under it. Tony looked at her with big eyes. He knew what time it was. He was about to go balls deep. Glow did things to Tony that he couldn't even imagine. He woke up the next morning to breakfast in bed. He was smiling like he had won the lottery.

Glow asked Tony, "What do you want to do for the day?"

"Glow, whatever you want to do. I'm with it."

Glow and Tony kicked it for about two months when she discovered she missed her period again. She knew she wasn't about to have another child and especially by this young kid she was sleeping with. She wasn't expecting for this little fling to go on as long as it did; she was just lonely at the time.

She decided to go to the drugstore to pick up a pregnancy test while Tony was out, to make sure she wasn't pregnant because if she was, she was going straight to the abortion clinic. She wasn't even giving Tony the satisfaction of thinking he was going to be a father, especially with her being the mother.

Glow didn't even know if Tony had children or not, and she didn't care Tony was only her playmate for now. When Tony made it back to Glow's house, she was still in the bathroom, waiting for the results from her pregnancy test. When he came in the door, he hollered her name to make sure she was still there. He had stopped by the store to pick up some roses for her.

Glow was so into what she was doing she didn't hear Tony call her name. She came out the bathroom without the pregnancy stick; she left it on the bathroom sink. She went back in the bathroom to get it when Tony turned to her. With the stick in his hand that read positive, she was in a state of shock because she was in her bedroom on the phone making an appointment to abort the baby.

Tony asked, "We having a baby?"

She said, "No, sweetheart, we're not."

Tony looked at Glow like she was sprouting two heads.

He said, "Yes, we are because I don't have any children at all."

Glow told Tony she wasn't trying to hear that because that's not her problem and that he could find someone else to be the mother to his children because she had her own child and that's all she needed.

Tony was devastated because for the first time in his life, he had a purpose and she wasn't going to take that away from him. Tony was so angry that he left Glow's house and didn't call her for two weeks. Tony was trying to convince Glow to have his child, not knowing that Glow had already aborted the baby. When Glow told Tony the baby was gone, he punched his fist through the wall and broke two of his knuckles; he was pissed.

Glow heard the noise and was scared. She really didn't think Tony would take it that hard, but he did. Tony was so angry with Glow until he started to have nightmares about a crying baby, and it drove Tony completely crazy.

Tony wanted to get back at Glow. He even thought about killing her daughter, but he fought himself against that thought, because Baby Girl didn't have anything to do with her mother's wrongdoings. He knew he was going to make Glow pay for getting rid of his child. He just had to come up with a plan to get close to her again because Glow stopped talking to Tony all together.

Glow tried to go on with her life. She even went to Aunt Marie's to get her daughter, and they were happy for a little while until one night she was coming home from Club Sexy. When she thought she was being followed, she kept looking out her rearview mirror. When she saw a black expedition following close behind her with bright lights, she started to speed up just to make sure she really was being followed this time. To her surprise, she was being followed by the mafia hit men. Mr. Salvador found out that Glow killed Silk, his inside source to her and her daughter. Glow was speeding so fast she missed her turn, so she went down a dark alley, pulled in someone's carport, and waited for the car to go pass.

After the car had passed and Glow saw it was safe for her to leave, she went home to call Tony. She hadn't talked to Tony in over three months because of the baby situation. Glow thought that she could at least get protection from Tony; he was the only one she could trust. Glow didn't know that Tony had moved over to the dark side; he was now working for Mr. Salvador.

If she only knew, when she called Tony, he was in the car with Mr. Salvador's hit man, Killer. Killer and the other bodyguards of Mr. Salvador's were the ones who killed Cane. Glow was in a world of trouble and didn't know the one she trusted the most was the one to bring her to her demise.

Tony answered Glow's call like he was glad to hear her voice. Deep down, he loved Glow, but she cut him deep when she got rid of his child. He couldn't forgive her for that. She asked Tony if he could come over.

She said, "It's something I have to talk to you about. Can you please come? It's an emergency."

Tony said okay and was on his way.

When Tony arrived at Glow's house, he asked her where her daughter was. She told him she was in her bedroom, asleep. Glow gave Tony the rundown on what had just happened. He wasn't in shocked because he knew he was behind it all. Tony had to clear his throat; since his mouth was dry, he needed water quickly, so he asked Glow to get him something to drink and she did. Glow went and got Tony a bottle of water. When she came back in the living room, she froze in her tracks.

Tony was standing there, right beside Killer, holding a knife up to her daughter's throat. She dropped the bottle of water and begged Tony not to kill her daughter: "Please, she has nothing to do with this."

Killer looked at Tony and said, "You handle your business with her, and I will be in the other room with her daughter."

Tony thought killing Glow was going to be easy. It was he who jumped forward and hit Glow in the face with a hammer. When she went down to the floor, she fell back on to a glass coffee table that split her back. She was still breathing when Tony bent over to check her pulse, so he took a guitar string and wrapped it around her neck until she wasn't breathing anymore.

Glow was dead, and Baby Girl whined up being raised by Mr. Salvador, head of the mafia, getting groomed to be a hustling diva, to run the Chicago area like her father suppose to have done. Before Killer left Glow's house with Baby Girl, wrapped in a blanket, he knew he wasn't going to leave Tony alive to tell the story of Glow's death or the kidnapping of Angel a.k.a. Baby Girl.

Killer took Baby Girl to the car. She was still sleeping and left her laying in the backseat asleep with the driver sitting up under the steering wheel, ready to hit the gas at any given notice. Killer already knew Tony was going in a blaze of glory. He loaded up the needle with heroin, and Tony closed his eyes only to see the vision of his mother who he never met before. Tony was dropped off on the doorstep of the hospital when he was only two weeks old, so Tony was all alone; he didn't have family anywhere. So it didn't matter to Tony what happened to him. He did think he had something to live for when he found out Glow was pregnant, but that went down the toilet with the shit.

Chapter Four
Angel a.k.a. Baby Girl

THE BEGINNING OF hustling diva; Baby Girl grew up in a house that was fit for a king. She was raised alongside her brothers: Cane's sons by his first wife Rakia, the mafia princess; her name had been changed to protect her innocence from the police looking for her after finding her mother brutally killed. The police had put out an all points bulletin to find Angel Carter.

What they didn't know was Angel was never going to be found under that assumed name, but she will show up in Chicago years later on a most wanted poster. Angel went to the most prestigious schools and graduated with honors; she drove the best cars and was spoiled rotten by her new family.

Her brothers loved her. They looked at her as being the most beautiful girl they knew beside their mother. All while she was going to school, she never got picked on because everyone knew Mr. Salvador wasn't anyone to play with, so she got royal treatment. She went to college with two friends she met in high school; they loved each other; they did everything together.

Gabriel was Italian and black; she was born into the mafia; her father, Mr. Giovanni, was the head of the Detroit area. She was spoiled rotten as well; she was five seven and had long curly hair and green eyes; she weighed a hundred and twenty-five pounds and had the prettiest smooth skin that Angel had ever seen.

Her other girlfriend name was Abby. She was mixed too: her father was white and her mother was black. She was taller than Angel and Gabriel. She stood six feet even and had long brown hair with green eyes; she had even skin. Abby could have been a twin sister to Jennifer Lopez, Abby's father was an ob-gyn doctor and her mother was a criminal attorney, so she was born in wealth as well.

21

Angel was very happy being the number one girl in the Salvador family. She came accustom to their way of living when she graduated from college. Mr. Salvador called a meeting with his granddaughter Angel and grandsons Dante and David had come of age to run the family business, and it was time for them to spread their wings.

Mr. Salvador had six buildings to run in Chicago: each one of the three children had two buildings apiece to run. When Angel, Dante, and David was all called down for dinner, they all were given assignments, but Angel didn't want to go without her friends. Angel went without her friends only to be joined by them six months later.

By the time Gabriel and Abby made it to Chicago, the threesome had Chicago on lock. David and Dante fell into the dope business like soldiers. The dope gang was a cakewalk to the twin boys. What scared the other dope boys on the set was how much they looked like Cane; it was like looking into a mirror. They were on top of the drug gang better than their father was because David was an accountant and Dante was deep into politics.

All three of them were groomed to make the money. And to not let the money make them, they were running drugs, guns, prostitution, black market babies selling, and all: whatever brings money in they did it. They even had a warehouse full of furs; they were getting rid of fur coats like lottery tickets.

Angel had to go to the airport to pick her girls up. When she rolled up to the drop-off curve, they were frozen in their tracks. She rolled up on them in a baby blue Rolls-Royce.

Abby said to Angel, "Damn! Girl, they haven't started making those yet."

Angel said, "You have to know somebody who know somebody girl."

What they didn't know was when Angel touched down in Chicago, she hit the ground running. She knew just how to run their organization. She and her twin brothers used to meet once a week to compare notes to make sure all of them was on the same page. They didn't have to stay in touch with Mr. Salvador but once a month, and after that, it was only once every six months they were to call only if they were in trouble.

Dante and David ran their businesses like clockwork. They had to hire madams for their whorehouses; they would go to top-notch private parties, where there were top-notch call girls that they knew they could hire to be madams. The women there were gorgeous and had the know-how to be what they wanted them to be; if not, they had already put plans in motion to have them trained to be the best madams Chicago area had ever seen.

Dante put an attorney on retainer when they made it to Chicago just in case they needed one. Dante didn't know they were going to become best friends, but what Dante didn't know that the attorney he put on retainer was as shiest as they come. He also had his hand in a little bit of everything. Mike Trivet was a black attorney who fought his way through law school; he even killed a couple of people to get there.

Growing up poor in the hood gave him his brownie points. He did his dirt on the low so no one would find out about it. He wasn't married, but he had two sons by two different women from previous relationships. He wasn't seeing anyone exclusive right now; he was just playing the field for a while until he ran into Miss Right.

Mike Trivet was a tall, handsome, clean-cut guy with a low-cut fade and beautiful hazel green eyes. He was born and raised in the Lower West Side of Austin, Texas. His mother died of a drug overdose when he was twelve, and his grandmother raised him until she died of a stroke when he was eighteen years old.

Leavening him to the streets, he never knew his father because his grandmother didn't like his father, so she never let him come around Mike. When Dante first met Mike, they were at a convention for lawyers. Dante was there to pick and choose; he wanted someone with a little swagger. Dante saw Mike in the meeting, and something about him stuck out like a sore thumb. Dante kept saying to himself, *This guy looks familiar. He looks like we could be related.*

After the first encounter with Mike, Dante knew he had to be on his payroll, and he also knew that David and Angel had to meet him as well because they all had to agree on Mike being their attorney, and he hoped that they would see what he was seeing because he could be related for real.

Dante set a dinner date with the three of them and Mike for them to get to know Mike. When they arrived at the restaurant, they were in an awe too because he looked so familiar to them as well, but they couldn't place him, so they left it a long for now. Angel's two friends came with her to dinner, and they were mesmerized at how sexy Mike was. They didn't know who was going to holler at Mike, but they knew one of them was going to give Mr. Trivet a run for his money.

That evening, the meeting went well, and they all agreed to keep Mike on retainer, because their grandfather, Mr. Salvador, told them once they made it to Chicago, they had to act like they weren't any kin to or had ties to the mafia family, period. So they had to pretty much handle their own affairs.

Unless it was a life-and-death situation that was the only way they can come in contact with him, but other than that, they did mafia business through Killer and Killer only. Angel's twenty-third birthday was coming up, and Dante and David were planning a big birthday bash for her at Club Sexy, the hottest club in the tri-state area. They wanted to do it big for their little sister, so they hired her favorite singer Keyshia Cole to perform at her party as a surprise.

David let Angel's friends, Abby and Gabriel, in on the surprise so they can keep her occupied for the day. David told them to take her to the shopping and to the spa, which will make her happy; she wouldn't say no to that as Angel liked to shop.

Abby said, "Stop playing, twin. Don't every female like to go shopping?"

David reached in his wallet and pulled out a black MasterCard with a two-hundred-thousand-dollar limit and said, "Go crazy. Make my sister look like the princess she is."

While David was taking care of Angel, Dante was over at Club Sexy, getting it set up for the party that night. He took care of the music, and now he was working on the decorations.

Dante didn't know any decorators, so he had to call Mike to see if he knew any. Mike told him yes, and he would have someone at Club Sexy in twenty minutes, so that part was over and Dante could breathe again. By the time Abby, Gabriel, and Angel were done shopping and going to the spa, it was time to get the party started.

Gabriel had to think of a master plan to get Angel out of the house for the party, especially since Angel said she was tired and wanted to take a nap. Gabriel had two hours to get Angel to her own surprise birthday party. All three girls had three-thousand-dollar gowns with two-thousand-dollar matching shoes and handbags.

They knew they were going to be the shit at Club Sexy even though Angel didn't know they had plans on going out for the evening. When Angel woke up from a thirty-minute sleep, Abby and Gabriel had already had their showers and were flat ironing each other's hair, because they didn't have enough time to get to the beauty salon; it was all right because the two girl's had natural straight hair.

They finally got Angel to agree to go to the club with them, and they all looked gorgeous coming into the club; they had all eyes on them. When Angel walked in the club, the people that were there started singing surprise. She broke down crying, because she thought her brothers had forgotten about her birthday because they didn't even acknowledged her birthday at all that day.

The party was kicked off in high gear when the big, bright light lit up on stage, and Angel didn't know what was going on until they announced coming to the stage is Keyshia Cole, and Angel really broke down. Dante thought he was going to take her to the emergency room, but she was out of it. She thanked her brothers over and over for loving her so much.

Chapter Five
Terror and Destruction

AFTER THE PARTY, it was time to get down to business. Angel had two shipments of cocaine coming in the next morning. She had to get her crew of soldiers assemble, and she wanted nothing but the best, so she decided she would go out and recruit a badass team of soldiers by having them trained by undercover police officers: going to shooting ranges and teaching them how to handle high-powered weapons with silencers and scopes and night vision goggles.

She wanted her soldiers to be well-equipped and unstoppable. She wanted them all to wear bulletproof vest. She also had two judges, police officers, detectives, and the prosecuting attorney in her pocket as well. She had Chicago on lock. Now that she had her players all in line, it was time to put Chicago in terror and destruction.

Her second order of the day was to call Killer to line up fifty terrifying guys from all sides of the world because she was building an empire from the ground up. She knew she was bred by the head of a mafia family, and she wanted her grandfather to be proud of her and her brothers. Angel made one more call to her brothers. She was hanging up the phone from talking to Killer when she saw on television this most wanted photo of this black guy named Cortez Smith a.k a. Killer Perez; he was wanted for a triple murder. It was something about him that struck a nerve in Angel. He had a mug that would scare a dead person, and she knew she had to have him as one of her soldiers.

Angel had to come up with a way to have him located; no matter what the cost was, she wanted him found. She hired an investigator to hunt him down; he charged Angel two thousand dollars an hour which she accepted. She left

Deacon Hayes's office with a smile on her face because she heard he was a good investigator from Mike. Mike told Angel he could find a pinhole in cotton.

Angel had two weeks left to assemble her troop of soldiers. Killer contacted Angel to let her know he had her team on the their way in a week, so Angel put her call into the police officers she had on payroll to be on standby when they were ready.

She said, "Cool, I will give you guys a call in a week."

Dante and David were on the other side of town assembling their soldiers as well. They agreed to have undercover retired police officers to be their soldiers, and they put a lot of thought in their plan. Dante asked Mike what he thought about their decision. Mike told him to go for it. ("What could they lose? They were already trained and knew the streets like the back of their hands.") Plus Mike knew just the guys they needed.

Dante and David set up a meeting with Mike and the retired police officers to see if they are down with being soldiers for the dark side. When they got to the meeting, the retired officers were shocked to see how much the two guys looked so familiar to this missing Hawaiian kingpin Cane Carter. But they didn't let it bother them because they needed the money if the price was right. Dante and David agreed to settle on an allotment of two thousand dollars a week, because they had to protect the drugs houses and the whorehouses. David and Dante needed one chief in command, so to pick a true soldier, they put the ten guys through a few test.

Dante and David wanted the guys to kill their firstborn child to prove his worth to them; they didn't care about the guys or their families because they had an empire to run and would kill crawling babies if they got in the way. It was this one officer they called Hammer that was crazy as hell. He had three sons that were as crazy as he was; they stayed in trouble all the time. His firstborn child Montello was a vindictive son of a bitch that hated Hammer with a passion.

So it wasn't going to be a problem with Hammer sending his firstborn child to hell. The other officers told Dante and David that they were two sick individuals and to go straight to hell, but Hammer didn't; he stayed on board because he really was a sick individual for real.

For Dante and David to be sure Hammer was going to go through with what they asked him to do, they sent Mike along with him, and he was to bring back the head of his firstborn child, and they also wanted pictures and his birth certificate with Hammer's government name on it as being his biological father.

The twins meant business; they were taking no shortcuts; it was all about their empire, and nothing or no one was going to get in their way. When Hammer returned that evening, he had his son's head wrapped up in a plastic bag down inside a box. He did what he set out to do, and he did it with no remorse. The twins loved it; they knew they had a crazy ass lunatic on their team, but they also knew to keep a watchful eye on his crazy ass.

Meanwhile, on the other side of town, Angel had her soldiers as promised, and they were in training. Angel and her girls were headed to the military store to purchase over a hundred bulletproof vests, and they were so sexy when they walked up in the store; she knew her plan to get the artillery she wanted was going to go off with a bang.

Two days later, Angel had set up one of her building strictly for pregnant runaway teens. She was getting ready for her black market baby-selling business. She had already peeped out four teens she became friends with and let them move into her building because they had nowhere else to live.

Angel took real good care of the girl as for as feeding and clothing and making sure they kept all doctor's appointments. They were glad they weren't living pillar to post anymore. They really thought Angel was their friend. What they didn't know was Angel had planned to sell their babies to the highest bidders on the black market.

Amy, Dina, Alexandra, and Cynthia were close friends; they all were pregnant living on the streets until they met Angel coming out of a grocery store one day. They thought Angel felt pity for them, but Angel had her own agenda for them. Angel took them home with her that day and put them up in one of her building for safekeeping.

Amy, Alexandra, and Cynthia had four more months to go before they delivered their babies, but Dina was due any day know, and Angel already had her website up and running and had their pictures and health reports already printed out for the expected parents to view. She knew what each girl was having, and the expected parents were waiting for their child's arrival.

Angel was selling each child for a hundred thousand dollars a pop; she was getting her money back for taking care of the girl's room and board and their expensive doctor bills. The terror began on a hot summer night of July when Dina went into labor. She was screaming so loud she woke up the other girls, but Angel made them go back to bed; she said she could handle it.

Angel took Dina downstairs in the basement, where she had it set up like emergency room for delivering babies; it came equipped with every tool the physician used to deliver babies. Angel even had a doctor on staff, but he wasn't an ob-gyn doctor, so he didn't know anything about delivering babies.

Angel didn't care. She just wanted the babies. She didn't care about the babies' moms, and she just wanted the babies to be born healthy. Angel knew the babies' mothers' wasn't going to make it out the house of hell when she let them move in. Dina's baby was having problems coming down in the canal; he was breached, so the doctor had to think of something quick. The doctor pulled Angel out in the hallway and told her he didn't know what else to do.

Angel said, "What the hell do you mean? You're a damn doctor, aren't you?"

The doctor said, "Yes, I specialize in gunshot wounds, not delivering babies."

Angel got so angry. Without thinking, she took a scalper and cut the doctor's throat, leaving Dina on the delivery table bleeding to death. Angel heard her scream out in pain, so she took that same scalper and cut Dina stomach open and took out the baby.

She took the baby and wrapped him in a blanket and put him in the baby bed while she checked on Dina. When she saw the look in Dina's eyes, she knew she was half-dead anyway, so she took the drill on the table and cut Dina's head off. She started cutting Dina's body into little pieces.

The baby started to cry, and Angel didn't know what to do, so she picked the baby up and gave him a bottle of milk she had prepared in the refrigerator. He stopped crying. Angel called her girlfriends to let them know that one of the babies was born and the mother died during childbirth.

Angel didn't want them to know that she was a born killer just yet, but they would know in due time. Dina's roommates wanted to know what happened to her and her baby, so they asked Angel when she came in that morning. Angel told them that Dina took her baby and moved back home with her mother because she didn't want to raise her child alone.

Three days after Dina's disappearance, Cynthia asked the other two girls, "Don't you guys think that's odd that Dina went back home to her mother's? When we were living on the streets, remember, Dina saying her mother dying in a house fire."

They all sat and thought for a minute and said, "You're right. Something's not right, and we need to find out what really happened to Dina."

The months were passing fast and the girl's bellies were bursting out at the seams. They went into labor four days behind each other, and the same procedures were done, except for Amy. She wasn't about to come up missing. Later that night, she went into labor first, but her labor pain was fifteen minutes apart. Amy got up and snuck out of the house. She wanted her baby, and she didn't want to whine up like Dina, so she ran as fast as she could until she passed out in front of a grocery store.

When Amy came to, she was in the hospital. She gave birth to an eight-pound-ten-ounce little boy who she named Conner. She never talked to anyone about what happened in the house of hell. She never saw Alexandra or Cynthia again.

Amy never left town. She got herself together and got a job at a printing shop and became a manager in no time. She was putting new signs around the store when she heard a gentleman's voice behind her say "Excuse me, could you help me please?" When Amy turned around, she almost fainted because he was so handsome.

She said, "Hi, my name is Amy."

The guy said, "Hi, my name is David."

David and Amy exchanged numbers, and David ordered a hundred of army fictive uniforms for his soldiers. David gave Amy a call for a dinner date and she accepted. David told Amy that he would pick her up at eight thirty for their dinner date, and she said she would be ready and gave David her address.

David and Amy had a wonderful dinner. They shared decent conversation, and they kept staring into each other's eyes. They both needed to be in each other's company. David was stressed out with running his empire, and Amy was worried that she might run into Angel on the streets, but she needed a breath of fresh air too.

David and Amy were going hot and heavy for a couple of months when Angel decided to give an introduction dance for their soldiers. When Angel notice this female entering the room with David, her heart almost popped out of her chest. She knew her eyes had to be playing tricks on her. *That can't be Amy on the arm of my brother. I have to get her to meet me in the bathroom because she bet not tell my brother she knows me.*

Amy looked shocked to know David knew Angel because out of the two months they've been together he didn't say anything about his family at all. Angel went to the bathroom first and Amy followed behind.

Angel said, "Long time no see."

Amy said, "Same here."

Angel's next question put fear in Amy.

"How do you know my twin brother David?"

"Is David your brother? I had no idea that you two were related."

"Now that you do, I need you to step off because if you don't, I would run your whole life history down to my brother. Do you honestly think that a man of his caliber would want a low-life trap like you."

"Angel, relax. It's not like I'm trying to marry him. I'm Just having a little fun with him like men being doing to women for years."

Angel grabbed Amy around the neck and whispered in her ear and told her, "Bitch, if you don't dismiss my brother, you will be dead in twenty-four hours," which sent chills down Amy's spine because she still have nightmares about the night Dina disappeared.

Amy stilled dated David on the low. She wouldn't go to none of the family dinners. She always would make up excuses. David never questioned Amy. He just thought that she was a sickly person because if it wasn't her period, she had very bad headaches.

But one time in particular, David wanted her to go to a football game with him, Dante, and Angel and her friends. He had bought the tickets a month early so they all could go together, but once again, Amy came up with another illness. She told David that her son had the chicken pox, and she couldn't leave him with the babysitter because she had children too.

David understood her concept with the chicken pox theory because he and Dante caught them at the same time, so he agreed that she needed to stay home with her son, but deep down Amy hated the fact that Angel had her head in a vice grip hold. She was going to make Angel pay for ruining her happy time with David.

Angel planned on making Amy's life a living hell because Amy ran from the house with her baby before Angel could kill her and take her baby. In Angel's mind, Amy made her miss out on a hundred thousand dollars, and Angel knew that Amy's child would be a hot commodity; her son was mixed with black and Cherokee. She had a couple that was mixed with the same blood and their willing to pay the price Angel agreed upon.

Angel found out where Amy stayed, and she had her house watched for weeks without her knowing it. What Amy didn't know was that the path of destruction was on its way. Angel was planning on kidnapping her son and transporting him to Washington DC. She didn't want to hurt her brother. That's why she had Killer to have David to come pick up the packages this time. That way David would be out of town when the kidnapping went down.

Angel had Amy so afraid that she couldn't sleep at night. She knew once Angel saw her again, she was going to have hell to pay, but she didn't want David to know about her relationship or her involvement with Angel.

David really liked Amy a lot. He knew something wasn't right between Amy and his sister. He could tell the first time he took her to their house for dinner, but he decided to let it go for now to a later date.

David left town two days later to pick up their packages. They didn't trust anybody but themselves or Killer to make the trafficking runs.

But sooner or later, David was going to see why Amy feared his sister. He knew she feared her because he was holding Amy's hand when they walked into the family dinner, and Amy's palms had started to sweat and her face went beet red like she had seen a ghost. Everyone in the room could feel the tension.

The saga continues. Stay tuned to David finding out about Angel kidnapping Amy's son.

Chapter Six
An Affair with Mike Trivet

MIKE WAS AT his office when he got a phone call from Angel. She wanted to meet with him about getting a safe made into her bedroom floor. She tried to call her brothers to get the information she needed, but they were in a meeting with some bankers so she didn't want to disturb them, but she wanted to see Mike anyway because he ran through her mind a lot, and she wanted to know why so going to his office was right up her alley.

When Angel made it to Mike's office, he was sitting behind his handcrafted big mahogany desk. The man was wearing a tailor-made navy blue Armani suit. Angel said, *Damn! I know he spent a grip on that suit, but I'm with it.* Mike sat back in his seat, looked Angel straight in her eyes and said, "What can I do for you today, pretty lady?"

Angel told Mike that she wanted to know if he could recommend anyone he could trust to put a build in safe in her bedroom floor.

Mike said, "Of course I do. Me."

She told Mike to quit playing. She wanted someone that was licensed and bonded.

He told, "Angel, I don't have those credentials, but I've learned how to put in safes. You think I went to school just to be a lawyer?

"Girl, I went to street school. That's where I got my credentials to put in safes and to be a locksmith as well."

Angel looked at Mike and said, "Oh, you got jokes. I tell you what, funny man come by my house tomorrow, bring the safe, and I will be the judge of what you can do, all right."

Mike took Angel up on her invitation and was at her house on time with the safe the very next day because quite as kept Mike had his eyes on Angel too.

31

Angel made sure when Mike got to her house, she had plans in motion to cook dinner, have some wine on chill, and serve herself up as dessert. She left Mike's office that day and went to Victoria's Secret to buy her a nice and nasty nightgown of her choice. She also saw this hot pink number that she wanted with the bra and panties to match. She wanted her first time to be special. Mike didn't know it was her first time, but he would soon find out.

When Mike arrived at Angel's house, he smelled this aroma coming out of her door before he rung her doorbell. He said to himself, *Damn! Something sure do smell good. I wonder what it is, and I hope she invite me to dinner because a brother sure is hungry.* To his surprise, Angel came to the door wearing nothing but that hot pink pantie and bra set she had just picked up from Victoria's Secret. She had on a pair of five-inch stilettos hot pick. Mike was looking at Angel like she was cotton candy on a stick, and he was ready to devour her like she was a steak with steak sauce.

Mike and Angel sat down and ate dinner, and for the main course, she told Mike to come into the bedroom where she wanted her floor safe to be, and when Mike opened Angel's bedroom door, she lay across her bed on a white mink blanket buck naked, with red rose petals floating across the mink blanket. Mike almost passed out; he told Angel she was the sexiest woman he had ever seen.

They made love all night. That was the beginning of a love affair between Mike and Angel. The next morning, when Mike left Angel's house to go to work, Angel decided to give her girls a call. She had been neglecting them for the last three days, and they wanted to know what Angel was hiding.

Angel really had to get a mind-set to tell her girls what really was going on because she knew they both had their eyes on Mike Trivet. Lying back in the shadows secretly, Angel knew she was going in for the kill. She was going to get Mike's attention without her girls, knowing she was going behind their back to have an affair with him.

The affair was getting so intense she thought that she had to let the cat out of the bag. Abby and Gabriel knew Angel was devises, but they had no idea she was cutthroat. If she had let her girls know what her intentions was on the situation with Mike, she would have known that Mike the shiest attorney was secretly seeing Gabriel.

Why she didn't acknowledge the fact that Mike never asked her out to dinner and to invite her to his apartment was beyond me. Angel invited her girls over to her house for lunch. She had her chef to prepare smoke salmon and grilled vegetables and garlic bread sticks, and to chill some mascot. Angel also said it was a nice day, so she wanted a table set up on a balcony.

When the girls made it to Angel's house at one thirty, they hugged each other like they usually did. They haven't seen each other in a couple of days. They all reached for a glass of wine from the table and made their way to the balcony. They sat down at the table and said grace, and they all started to eat lunch. Abby started the conversation by telling the girls about her new guy. She told them he was tall, dark, and handsome, and that he was self-employed; he ran his own business as a caterer.

Angel and Gabriel were so excited for Abby because she was always saying she was homesick, and they wanted her to get out more and meet people. So when Gabriel started to say something, her phone started ringing. She said, "Hold up you guys. This is my man."

Angel and Abby were shocked because they didn't know she was seeing anyone since the day they arrived in Chicago, so to even know she had a sidekick was a plus.

When Gabriel made it back on the balcony, they started asking her question about her gentleman caller. Gabriel was told by Mike to keep their relationship a secret for now until he was ready for everyone to know and Gabriel agreed. What Gabriel didn't know was Mike was banging Angel's brains out on a regular basic. Angel still had not, made her mind up to tell the girls about her relationship with Mike either, but she did make up a man for the time being. Angel told her girls that she was seeing one of her brothers' associates. They were like "Girl, you know the rules. Never mess around with your brothers' friends or associates."

Gabriel asked Angel, "Which one of your brother's friend was it, Dante's or David's?"

Angel asked Gabriel, "Why?"

Gabriel said, "I was just asking."

But what Gabriel really wanted to know was is it Mike, but Angel didn't say it was Mike, but also didn't say it was. So to come up with a quick lie, Angel told them, "His name is Donovan, a guy David just hired to be his right-hand man."

Angel got away with her mischievous ways for now, but her lies will catch up with her sooner than she thinks. Mike called Angel soon after Abby and Gabriel left. He knew they were leaving because he had just invited Gabriel over to his place to watch a couple of movies with him. Gabriel was excited; she loved being in the company of Mike. He would give Gabriel lap dances and massages with warm oils and would set Gabriel's soul on fire.

That night, Angel lay in bed thinking about that sex session she had with Mike the night before. The tension was so strong until Angel reached to her nightstand draw and pulled out her friend she called Big Mike. Angel lay there in bed sexing herself while Mike was cross town knocking boots with her best friend Gabriel.

The next morning, when Gabriel left Mike's apartment, he jumped in the shower. When Mike got out of the shower and got dressed to go to work, he made a phone call to Angel to tell her how much he missed her last night, but he was really tired and needed some rest. Mike asked Angel did she want any company when he got off work. She told Mike she had a lot of errands she had to make, but he could give her a call later that evening. Mike said cool and they hung up. A few minutes later, Mike's office door flew open and in came Abby, dressed in a trench coat with nothing on up under it.

Mike was a bad boy; he was screwing all three of them, and they didn't have a clue. Mike asked Abby did they believe her when she told them about her guy. She told Mike they did. But she told him, "I don't like lying to my friends. Why can't I tell them that we've been an item since Angel's birthday party?"

Mike told Abby she couldn't let anyone know that they were dating because of the rules: you never date friends or coworkers Abby believed Mike, so she was all right with it for now. Abby looked at Mike and dropped her coat to the floor; they had sex on the desk, the floor, and even in Mike's windowsill. They screwed all over Mike's office like rabbits in heat.

Mike had all three of the girls falling for his game. He knew this wasn't going to work for long. His head was swimming with lies and desires to have them all, but he did know his plan was heading for a disaster, plus he was having unprotected sex with all of them. His plan was to get them pregnant with his daughter and dump them. He wasn't ready for a permanent relationship.

Mike loved all three girls' mixed complexions, and he wanted a daughter as gorgeous as the three of them were. What Mike didn't know was they were gorgeous and deadly and he was going to pay a high price if they ever found out that he was playing them against each other. Mike went out that night with his office secretary on a business meeting for the next day.

Mike wasn't in Mike mode like he normally be, looking over his shoulders this particular evening. When Angel wasn't feeling the lie he told her earlier, so she thought that she would go sit outside his office building to see what was up with Mr. Mike Trivet. While she was sitting in her car, she lit a Black & Mild and inhaled, and when she blew the smoke out of her lungs, Mike came out his office with this beautiful woman, which upset the shit out of Angel, so she followed close behind Mike: when he made a right turn, she made a right turn as well.

When Mike and his female companion arrived at their destination, Angel was hot on his trail. She asked for a table in the corner in the back part of the restaurant so she couldn't get spotted. When she saw Mike reach over the table and kiss this woman, she almost fell out of her chair. Angel said to herself, *Hold on, Baby Girl. The ball is in your court now. All you have to do is let it play itself out, Baby Girl.*

Angel was shocked when Baby Girl came out of her mouth. That name Baby Girl, she kind of remembered someone calling her Baby Girl. Angel was so devastated about her mind playing tricks on her until she almost forgot what she was doing and why she was hiding in a corner in the back of a restaurant, and when she noticed Mike and his date exiting the restaurant, she made her way out of the restaurant two feet behind them. He still didn't notice Angel behind them. Angel was so close behind them, and if she was a snake, she could have put venom in both of them.

Mike dropped off his date at home and kept on moving. Angel continued to follow Mike so she could give him a piece of her mind, but once he pulled up in his parking lot, Angel decided to wait until the time was right, so Angel drove on home, but her mind was in high gear. She thought she heard someone say Baby Girl, and she was frightened shitless, and she couldn't wait to get home so she could get her a glass of wine and settle down her nerves.

Once Angel arrived home, she opened her front door and ran down her long hallway to the bathroom. She had to use it bad she had been holding her piss the whole time she was in the restaurant. Angel couldn't believe she was being that petty she said to herself, *Angel, don't chase men, they chase me.* Before Angel could get in the shower, Mike was ringing her phone and telling Angel that he just came in from work and if she was up to any company. Angel dismissed his thoughts before he could say another word. She said, "I'm sorry, baby. I have company right now, so can we hook up tomorrow?"

After Angel hung up the phone with Mike, she took her shower and went to bed alone, she thought but while she was sleeping, she had an occurring nightmare; she hadn't had a nightmare since she was nine years old, but this time it was different. She saw this man that favored her brothers and herself, and he also said "Baby Girl, you grew up to be a very beautiful woman. Not to be afraid I'm your father. I love you. I would never hurt you."

Angel's nightmares came so regular that she missed money because she couldn't sleep at night, so she decided to go see a therapist for help. When she arrived at the therapist Chloe Daniel's office, she was very scared because Ms. Daniel said she wanted to hypnotize Angel to get down to the bottom of her nightmares. Angel got relaxed on the sofa while Ms. Daniel got her watch and dangled it in her face. Ms. Daniel asked Angel to count to ten, and she would find herself finally going to sleep.

Angel fell into a deep sleep she started to moan and fight the sleep. She didn't want to see what she was seeing. Angel saw the murder of her mother. She saw Tony hit her mother in the face with a hammer. She didn't know who Tony was, but she knew who Killer was for sure. She also remembered going into this big house with electric gates, and when she made it to the inside of this big house, she was handed to an old man with cigar breath.

Angel was given to a nanny that night to get her dressed for bed, and when she woke up that morning, sitting in her bedroom was this beautiful woman, and she was told that Rakia was her mother and been six years old what was she suppose to think. She also was told that she had two brothers David and Dante. She met them at breakfast and loved them.

After Angel woke up from being hypnotized, she was wide awake. What Ms. Daniel didn't know was she had just created a monster. Angel was not about to forget anytime soon what happened to her mother. Angel thanked Ms. Daniel and made another appointment for the next two weeks.

After Angel's visit to the therapist office, she went into hiding for a while. She had to recollect her thoughts. After a month, Angel came out of hiding and was ready to get back on her grind, and she came back harder than before. She called Killer for a hundred kilos of cocaine and two pounds of heroin. She flew to Hawaii to meet Killer. Angel wanted to look the guy in the eyes who killed her mother.

The affair with Mike and Angel was at a standstill. She couldn't add more pressure to her plate; she wanted to tell Mike his time was up, but she met with Mike one last time before she dismissed him. Mike wasn't to be trusted, but she did want him to crack her back one more time. Before she ended the affair, Angel waited and called Mike two days later just to have sex, and he wanted more. Mike wanted to spend the night, and Angel wasn't having that, so she told Mike that their affair was nice but she has to move forward, and she hoped he understood, but if he didn't, she was going to put two in his head just for thinking she was stuck on stupid.

Chapter Seven
Angel on the Grind

ANGEL HAD HER soldiers assembled and ready for war. They were stationed at both her two properties; they had the properties surrounded. She had one of her buildings loaded with nothing but drugs; the whole first floor is where they collected money and counted it.

They had at least five people who were responsible for counting the money with the money machine. The tricky part was they had to do it stock buck naked. Angel trusted no one, and she made it known to all of her soldiers. They had to gain her trust and that's not going to be easy.   The second floor was where they cooked up the drugs, bottled them in valves, and disturbed them to the soldiers.

Angel's third floor was a crap house. She had card games, crap tables, pool tables, and even had casino slot machines hooked up on the third floor. She had at least ten soldiers guarding the third floor because the house averaged ten to twenty thousand dollars a night. Angel was making money hand over fist.

Her soldiers that were selling her drugs on the streets were bringing in forty thousand dollars a week. Angel and her brothers came to Chicago and took the city by storm. The other drug dealers wanted to know who they were. Some of them knew only by association with Cane, and they feared Dante and David because they showed no fear and they meant business.

Angel was so busy getting on her grind she forgot about her investigator Deacon Hayes. Angel gave him a call only to find out he had just got back in town, and he found her mark Killer Perez was staying in a hotel in San Diego, California. He had been there in hiding for the last two weeks. Mr. Hayes told Angel that Perez would be running out of money soon so she needed to fly out to San Diego and get on top of things before Mr. Perez disappears again.

Angel took Mr. Hayes's advice and got ready to fly out that night, but she wasn't leaving town without backup, so she decided to take two of her soldiers with her: Tin Tin and Pop Eye with their two chicks. They were crazy as hell; they popped the head off a gorilla one night while they were at the zoo because the gorilla threw shit on them. Angel and her soldiers took the plane out that night and made it to San Diego in two hours, and they went straight to enterprise to rent a car. After Angel rented an Impala, they headed straight to the hotel on imperial drive to room 212, where Mr. Hayes said Killer Perez stayed. When they got there, he wasn't in his room. He had left the room to go get him something to eat, and when Perez made it back to the room, he didn't notice he had company sitting in his room until he cut the lights on. He reached for his gun on his side, but he was too slow. Tin Tin had her nine-pointed to his head, so he lowered his gun and asked them what the hell did they want.

Angel looked at Perez, and he scared the shit out of her; he had scares all across his face and it looked like somebody tried to cut his throat. Angel pulled herself together, so she could tell Perez why she came to San Diego to find a killer she wanted in her crew. Perez thought she was crazy and didn't she know he was a triple murder.

After Angel explained what she wanted with Perez, he seemed to calm down a little, especially after she gave him the amount of money he will be making. Perez was all about making that paper, but he didn't know that Angel was going to be on him like flies on shit.

Angel and her soldiers made it back to Chicago with Perez as planned. She still wanted her soldiers to keep a watchful eye on the triple murder Perez. She went to her other building where she sat up the first floor with pregnant teens—she had about twelve girls staying there now, and she spent a lot of money keeping them with what they needed.

Angel spent a whole lot of time on the grind. She had a team of girl soldiers robbing dope boys. They had mapped out this drug dealer's house name, St. Louis. He had a badass mansion; he had two bodyguards that stood out front his house, and he had six bedrooms and three bathrooms. He had a bedroom that had a bed in the middle of his bedroom that went down in the floor. He had a hidden room up under the floor that no one knew about.

The hidden room had cameras and guns. He had his fortress equipped with enough guns to start a war with military men in Iraq. So in order for Angel soldiers to move in on St. Louis, they had to work from the inside out, so Angel had one of her female soldiers to become his maid. She went in through an agency so it wouldn't be so much of a background check.

St. Louis went through four applications that day, and Mia looked the part;

she was in her midforties, and she reminded him of his elder sister Monique. He knew why, so Mia got a called that day from St. Louis to meet him at his house the next day at ten that morning, and she was told not to be late.

Angel told Mia, "All right, we're in. I knew the first time I saw him at Club Sexy, he had some paper. I was told by Mike he had at least ten million. If Mike was correct, I'm going to cut him a million if this robbery goes off without any of my people getting killed."

Angel's plan was to feed St. Louis's arsenic a little at a time. They were going to do this robbery slow and easy. She didn't want him dead just yet. What Angel didn't know game recognize game when they saw St. Louis pepped Angel the night of her birthday party. He was just waiting until she finished what she had going on with Mike. He had been keeping a close eye on her because if St. Louis wanted her, he got what he wanted.

St. Louis had his right-hand man scoping out Angel the whole time. He wanted to make her his woman, but first he wanted to do his own investigation on her. He knew she wasn't from the Chicago area because he would have known everything he needed to know about her. That evening, St. Louis's right-hand man Richie reported to him that Angel was back in town and she had an army of soldiers ready for war, which put St. Louis on attack mode because everybody had been trying to get him.

St. Louis knew something was brewing, but he didn't know what, but he knew to keep his ear to the ground, and sooner or later, someone was going to snitch. St. Louis thought that he should go up to Club Sexy, where Angel's brothers hung out, just maybe someone knew what was going on. Maybe some of them, hoodrat bitches, knew what was about to pop off.

Angel had her female soldiers ready. Only thing they had to do was wait on Mia to give them a map of St. Louis's fortress. Angel, Abby, and Gabriel went to Club Sexy the same night St. Louis was up in there. He was in awe when he saw Angel walk through the door. He said, *Damn! That girl is finer than a thousand dollar bottle of wine.*

Angel and her girlfriends watched St. Louis's every move that night. Angel wanted to rob him but something was pulling on her heart strings about St. Louis too. He looked very enticing. She started having second thoughts about robbing him. She thought to herself, *Hell, I can make him mine and get his money that way.* Angel's mind was all over the place. She said to herself again, *Hell, no! We're going to take his fortune and laugh in his face after we do it.*

What Angel didn't know was St. Louis wanted her mind, body, and soul. She could have every dime he had, because every time he saw Angel, it made his heart skip a beat; she had that kind of control over him, and she didn't even know it. St. Louis found out a week later about Angel's history. He found out that Cane, the Hawaiian kingpin, was her father. He also knew that Gloria Black a.k.a. Glow was her mother. He knew Tony was the one who killed her mother.

St. Louis didn't want to use this information he found out about Angel to hurt her. He wasn't going to use it unless he had to. A month went by, and Angel told her female soldiers they had all the information they needed on St. Louis so it was time to make a move. They were to go in through a underground tunnel; this would put them exactly under his bed in the middle of the room. St. Louis had a button; they could push on the side of the wall to slide the bed back.

The safe that was holding the money was made inside of the fish tank, underneath the fish tank. No one knew that but St. Louis and the guy that designed it, and to this day, the guy that designed it doesn't breathe the same air as St. Louis does.

Angel and the soldiers were all geared up with their army fatigues and bulletproof vests. They were ready to enter St. Louis's fortress that night. They knew he wasn't there because Mia had called and said he was gone out to dinner with his female friend, but he was due back in two hours.

While St. Louis was out to dinner, Angel and her female soldiers were making their way through the tunnel. They had enough explosives to blow St. Louis's house off the map, but before they could set the explosive in the position on the wall, they heard the alarm system say "front door open." They almost shitted because they all had on watches and their timers set for two hours, but he made it back in an hour and a half.

Angel knew when to regroup and make their next move, a careful one. So they decided to leave St. Louis's house undetected, which blew Angel's mind when St. Louis came back from his date that early: either his date wasn't worth his time or she was a boring chick. But frankly, Angel didn't give a damn. She just wished that the chick had enough stamina to keep old boy happy for at least two hours damn.

Angel and her crew made it out of the tunnel undetected and made it back to their destination safely; she was pissed because they were so close to getting that ten million dollars she could taste it. Angel felt like it was though St. Louis knew they were going to hit his spot only if Angel knew the truth, Mia really got the job of being her soldier through St. Louis, Mia was put in Angel's fold to investigate Angel for St. Louis. She was St. Louis's younger sister Mecca a.k.a. Mia.

Mia had already wired her brother up on what was about to go down, and that's why he cut his dinner short. He wanted to stop Angel from the mistake she was about to make because if she had stolen from St. Louis, he will have to kill Angel, and his method of killing Angel would be to cut out her uterus and hang her ass from a flagpole in front of the police station for the whole world to see.

St. Louis didn't want that. He had other plans for Angel. He loved her gangsterism, but he just wanted her to be on his team. He knew she had potential and that made his dick hard, plus she was beautiful and had her own money that was more than a plus for St. Louis. Angel had struck nerves in St. Louis. He didn't even know existed, but he just had to figure out how to get a handle on Angel.

Angel had a major crush on St. Louis quite as kept this man had it going on more ways than one he had a body like a goddess and swagger that couldn't quit. Being only twenty-three, Angel had more maturity than a woman in her forties, so she was about her business. Angel though about forgetting about robbing St. Louis for now. Her black market baby-selling enterprise was failing because the girls weren't having their babies fast enough. So Angel decided to go another route. She talked to Mike about opening up a stripper club.

Mike said, "Why not? There's so many trifling women around here they would welcome your club with honors."

All Angel had to do was find a spot and come up with a name. She was sitting at home thinking when the name Sugar Daddies popped right in her head. She called Mike, and he loved it, and Mike already found her a spot five blocks from Club Sexy, and it was on and popping because Club Sexy never had any competition. She had about ten strippers interviewed for the job openings, and to Angel's surprise, those bitches were freaky as hell.

Angel had one girl that applied for the job to sit down on a beer bottle and suck it up her vagina like it was a suction cup. This other girl named Candy had a snake, the snake lick her kitty cat like it was a blow pop filled with cocaine. Angel thought the shit was disgusting, but they showed Angel they could work the shit out the dancing poles, so Angel hired all ten girls, because she was about making money. That's it! If those bitches didn't have no respect for themselves, she sure didn't.

Chapter Eight
Dante and David

DANTE AND DAVID were on their grind as well. Their building was off the hook; their drug houses were exclusive: they had people coming in their set up with invitation; they only played with the bigwigs, like politicians, lawyers, congressmen, judges, and they even had high-price call girls servicing their gentlemen callers. They got high on the first floors and got sexed on the second floors, and the third floor was where they had a camera crew set up for the blackmailing scam they had going on for the men that were married and had a lot to lose.

They had pictures and videotapes of every activity going on in each building. They had a video of one of the judges getting his freak on with a pit bull, and the congressmen wanted to dress up in drag and get screwed in the butt by a big black guy named Buck. Dante though that was some sick shit, but it brought the money in so he was cool with it. When the lawyer asked if he could get this Chinese woman, Dante said "yes, if the price is right."

The lawyer asked, "What's the price?"

Dante said, "A thousand dollars round-trip. If you don't know what a round-trip is, it's everything baby: pass go and beyond."

What happened next: Dante and David sent to the bathroom this lawyer who they called Dirty Old Man who wanted the Chinese girl to take her six-inch pumps and stick the hill of her shoe up his ass. After that, he wanted her to step on his family jewels with her heels as well. They had seen some sick shit, but that was over the top for them. They knew this would get them paid; they had to make sure all their tapes were numbered and dated.

Dante and David had opened up a restaurant that was open 24-7. They were making money over fist as well, and they even opened up two clothing stores as well: one of the stores was only fashion for women which they called Bottoms Up; the second store was unisex and had jewelry and everything and mad handbags for women, and it was laid out. Inside, they had a lounge fit for a princess, where they had musclemen waiting on women knowing their sizes soon they enter the store.

Dante had finally met a woman; he had been putting his love life on the back burner for a while until he started his business. Now that everything is going the way he wants it, it's time to have some fun. He met this woman called Abigail two weeks ago, but he never thought it was the right time to call her. He happened to be going into the grocery store, and he bumped right into her with his basket, and he turned around and said "oh, I'm sorry," but was in shocked when he saw it was the one and only Abigail Dawson.

Abigail was breathtaking. Dante wanted to take her out to lunch, but he was too nervous to ask her out. He said to himself, *Man, get a grip. She's just a beautiful woman. She's human just like you. Ask her. What can she say? Yes or no, period.*

Dante got himself together and asked Abigail out to lunch, and she accepted, and they went to his restaurant called The Sugar Shack.

While Dante was on his date with Abigail, David was across town with Amy, getting his sex on. He still hadn't told anyone he and Amy were still dating, especially to his sister. He still needed to know why they (Amy and Angel) were enemies. What David didn't know was he was going to find out very soon because Amy's son, Conner, was about to come up missing. Amy asked David what he wanted to do for the evening, and he said let me see. So he decided to go out for the night thinking she didn't want to go, but he asked anyway, and she accepted to go out, but she had to call the babysitter first, and she agreed to come over and sit with Conner.

David and Amy went out that evening, and Angel was sitting down the street with her crew when they left. Angel couldn't believe that Amy had lied to her about still seeing her brother David. When she seen David walk out that door with Amy, she almost choked because she warned Amy to dismiss her brother, and she didn't. So Angel thought to herself, *Maybe, when I kidnap her son, she will know not to play with me.*

Angel had her girls Abby and Gabriel to put some heroin in a needle so she could slip the babysitter a shot, not enough to kill her just a little to knock her out for a while, just long enough to kidnap Conner. They made their way through Amy's back door without the babysitter noticing. Once they were in, she was sitting on the couch asleep, so she didn't see them standing behind her.

Gabriel shot the babysitter with the heroin, and she was out for count for real, and she and Abby and Angel proceeded to Connor's room, where he was fast asleep. Angel picked up Conner and started down the hallway with Conner. Before Angel left Amy's house, she left a note stating, *Bitch, I told you not to play with me.*

When David and Amy made it back to her apartment, she noticed her babysitter was nodding in and out.

Amy said, "What the hell is going on? Wake up, Shelly, what's wrong with you?"

Shelly couldn't even speak. She told Amy she didn't know what was wrong with her she just felt dizzy. Amy ran down the hallway to see if Conner was in his bedroom. When she didn't see Conner in his room at all, she panicked; she screamed so loud David came running down the hallway so fast he almost fell.

All Amy could do was cry. She told David, "Not my son! He's all I have. Please! Find my son, please."

David felt so bad that he called in some favors because he felt that the kidnapping was in house and "if it was heads, we're going to roll for this one." David contacted Dante for help as well, so he put Hammer on the job, knowing he was a retired police officer. He wanted the best, and time was an issue as well, because Conner was born with a heart condition. Conner took heart medicine once a day.

Amy couldn't sleep. Conner had been gone for over forty-eight hours. He had already missed two shots, and she was worried to death about her son. David came over to Amy's house to let her know the results to finding Conner, which wasn't much because he hadn't found out anything as of yet. While David was there, Amy had a premonition she knew who kidnapped her son, and she just had to take her chances on telling David, and hoping David understand and if he didn't that's his lost because that was her past.

Amy explained every little detail to David about her and Angel, including the part of Angel killing Dina and the black market baby-selling enterprise she had going on. David was shocked to hear Angel was into selling babies. He knew they were into some deep shit, but babies weren't a part of the equation. He couldn't believe what he was hearing.

He told Amy, "Let me get back to you. I have to clear my head. I would be in touch soon if I hear anything about your son. I will call all right."

David was so messed up about what Amy had just dropped on him until he couldn't think straight; he called Dante to come meet him at their restaurant as soon as possible. He was so messed up about their sister killing pregnant teens and stealing their children until he was beginning to hate ever knowing Angel as their sister.

When Dante made it to where his brother was, David looked devastated.

Dante asked him, "Man, you look like you seen a ghost. Let your brother know what's up."

When they were raised, they were never taught to hurt children. Their mother wouldn't have it or their grandfather. They were ruthless, but children never play a part in the killings they committed.

When David told Dante what was going on with Amy and how Angel was involved, he was heartbroken. The way they looked at Angel now was in a different light. Their little sister had sold her soul to the devil. Angel was raised in the same house with them, and they wanted to know what happened to her. They were all in the Windy City to make money, but Sister Girl took it to a whole other level.

Angel had become scandalous, and she had also overstepped her bounds. She was messing with someone David cared about. He really wasn't about to let her get away with kidnapping Conner. He wasn't sure it was her, but David was close to finding out. Dante called David to let him know Hammer had information concerning Conner, and David was on his way to one of Angel's apartment building where Hammer and Dante were waiting on his arrival. When he made it to Angel's building, Hammer let Dante and David know he saw this Cherokee couple go into the building carrying a bag and a big teddy bear, but the couple haven't come out yet, so they stayed, parked outside to see what was up.

Ten minutes later, the couple came out of the building carrying Conner, and that's when the shit hit the fan. The couple didn't know why Hammer had a gun pointed at their head. David took Conner out of the couple's arms and headed to his car so he could take Conner back to his mother. After he left Amy's house, he got in touch with Dante and told him that they had to have a serious talk with Angel soon.

Angel was pissed as she watched what was unfolding outside her apartment building: her brothers and their right-hand man Hammer were taking two hundred thousand dollars out of her pocket. She knew this was going to be war. Dante and David set the stage, so it's going to be World War III popping off in the Windy City of Chicago.

Chapter Nine
The Love Connection

A NGEL WAS SITTING in the window of her apartment when she spotted this white Cadillac sitting on twenties passing her apartment. Angel noticed the Cadillac before but it didn't bother her now. It's beginning to raise her suspicions about this white Cadillac passing her apartment so much, and she also noticed that the Cadillac had tinted windows. She couldn't see who was driving it, but she did notice that the car would slow down when it got close to her apartment building. Angel had planned on finding out who was the owner of the white Cadillac with tinted windows.

Little did Angel know the white Cadillac she saw passed her house on a regular basis. Was the man that hunted her dreams every night she was so in tune with St. Louis until it drove her crazy. She knew he had power, but damn, he ran through her mind like her blood supply going through her veins. Angel thought to herself, *Maybe I need to get to meet with St. Louis to see what's up with him.*

That night, Angel decided to go down to Club Sexy alone because she knew if St. Louis was there, she could meet him without anyone knowing. She had to know why this man had her heart in turmoil. He was the last person that would float through her mind before she would go to sleep at night. Angel entered Club Sexy at eight thirty that night, and St. Louis wasn't there, so she sat at the bar and had a couple of drinks. The bartender kept telling Angel she favored someone that used to own the club.

Eric the bartender asked Angel, "Did you know anyone by the name of Gloria Black a.k.a. Glow?"

Angel told Eric, "I didn't know her."

Eric said, "You and her could be twins. I swear you guys could be twin sisters."

Angel had two drinks and was getting ready to leave when she saw St. Louis walk in.

She said to the bartender Eric, "Let me get another apple martini please."

Eric handed Angel her drink, and she looked off like she didn't see the man of her dreams walk in the door. Angel was so excited when St. Louis walked in the door until her panties got wet just by looking at him.

Angel didn't want to seem too eager, so she acted like he was just another groupie, so Angel sat at the bar drinking until St. Louis spotted her sitting alone at the bar. He made his way over to the bar to put in a order of Crown Royal with a water back. Angel said to herself, *Damn! This man smells like a million bucks.*

St. Louis sat and watched Angel for an hour before he decided to get up and make the first move. He felt his heart strings pulling in his chest just like Angel did that night, so he manned up and walked toward Angel and introduced himself as Ronald Louis a.k.a. St. Louis.

Angel said, "Hi, my name is Angel Salvador. Nice to finally meet you." Angel told St. Louis that she had seen him in Club Sexy before, but he was always surrounded by his bodyguards.

St. Louis was so intrigued with Angel he had to ask her what was she mixed with. She told him Hawaiian and black.

He said, "Little mama, you are a very sexy woman, and now that we are alone, can I take you to dinner?"

Angel said, "Of course you can, only if I can choose the restaurant."

He said, "Cool. Or I can take you to my spot and have my chef to cook for us."

Angel said, "Let's go to your spot then."

But before they left Club Sexy, St. Louis wanted to call home to make sure Mia was in her room for the night.

St. Louis didn't get an answer from Mia, so he called her cell phone. She was on the grind for Angel, so it was safe to take Angel to his spot. St. Louis really wanted to let Angel know how he had his crib on lock. It wasn't going to be easy getting into his fortress. St. Louis went into his kitchen to get them a bottle of wine to drink before dinner to living them up a little more, and he even had plans on dropping his bomb on Angel about her trying to rob his fortress, but he had to use his words wisely. He didn't want to scare her off even before their love connection began.

Angel didn't know what was going to happen with her and St. Louis, but she knew for sure something was brewing. She could feel the butterflies in her stomach when he took her by her hand. He waited for dinner to be served before he dropped his bomb on Angel. He wanted her to feel comfortable in his presence first. Angel felt so comfortable around St. Louis until when he came back into the den. She had taken off her shoes. St. Louis knew that was a good sign because women don't take their shoes off in a man's house unless they feel safe enough to do so. After they were served dinner, St. Louis thought it was time to shed some light on Angel about the mistake she was fend to make if she had robbed his fortress.

St. Louis dismissed the chef for the night, and he and Angel chilled in the den around the lit-fire place. Angel felt a talk coming on from St. Louis because he sat across from her, holding her hand and looking deep into her eyes. She got so nervous until she started to sweat. Angel dropped her head so she didn't have to look St. Louis in his big brown eyes while he talked to her.

St. Louis took his hand and lifted Angel's chin up to his face and said, "Why are you so nervous? We have to be friends first before we can connect to an emotional level."

Angel was quiet at first because she knew St. Louis was talking real talk. It wasn't bullshit, so she was willing to listen to anything he had to say. What he said next sent cold chills through Angel's body.

He said, "Angel, I want you to know first that I like you a lot, and I love your gangsta you down for yours and that's a plus, but a gangster like me rock niggers to sleep about minds and you were about to cross the line when you and your soldiers thought that you were going to rob my fortress."

Angel looked like a deer caught in headlights when St. Louis spit that game out his mouth. Angel was truly shocked, and she wanted to get up and leave because she honestly thought it was a setup.

Once Angel knew it wasn't a setup, she calmed down a little. She said to herself, *This man must really like me or something because if I had a gangster in my camp that was thinking about robbing me, that person would be swimming with the fishes.*

But Angel knew she defiantly had to find out who was the snitch in her camp because someone was going to die.

Angel and St. Louis made a love connection that night. They talked for hours. Angel wanted to make love to St. Louis, but he wanted to get to know Angel. In his mind he could have sex whenever he wanted to. He had chicks lined up to get with him, but he didn't want them. He wanted Angel. Angel stayed at St. Louis's house all night. When the chef got there the next morning, he prepared breakfast for them both and then St. Louis dropped Angel back down to Club Sexy, where she left her car. But before they left, she noticed the white Cadillac sitting in his garage, and she said, *Oh, he's a stalker as well.* But it wasn't that St. Louis was being a stalker, it was him who was keeping an eye on his investment.

When Angel got dropped off at Club Sexy to get her car, she had no idea that her brothers would be sitting up in her ride. They had been trying to contact Angel, but she had been sending all their calls to her voice mail. She knew what they wanted, and she also knew their encounter wasn't going to go well, especially after the way they played her.

Dante was the first one to speak to Angel. "You know you have gone overboard, don't you? You have taken earning money to a whole other level. I and David think you need to step down."

Angel looked at David and Dante and said, "Are you two punks crazy? I was sent here to get paid just like the two of you, and if yawl don't back the hell up off me, there will be repercussion for real."

David was so upset that he reached over the seat and slapped the shit out of Angel. Angel tried to pull her gun out her purse to pop two in David's head when Dante stepped in and snatched the gun from Angel. He looked at her and said, "Have you lost your damn mind or what? Have hustling got you so far gone that you willing to kill your own brother."

Angel looked at Dante with bloodshot eyes and said, "We being related? Don't live here no more. You two half-breed motherfuckers have just started a war."

The next day, Angel woke up hoping she was dreaming but she wasn't. She still had the slap mark on her face that David left there. She couldn't forget the fact that her brother put his hands on her, and she was going to see to it that he never disrespect her again. David and Dante had to be dealt with soon.

While Angel was sitting there thinking about her brothers, the phone rang, snapping out her thoughts. When she picked up the receiver and said hello, it was St. Louis. He wanted to make dinner plans with Angel. She heard his voice and her butterflies started flip-flopping in her stomach again. Angel thought to herself, *I have to get closer to this man so I can get deep in his heart.*

Angel asked St. Louis, "Where do you want to eat?"

He said, "Wherever you like to dine, sweetie."

Angel and St. Louis had dinner at an Italian restaurant of her choice, and they really enjoyed each other's company until St. Louis saw the slap mark in her face. He was so pissed.

He asked Angel, "Who put their hands on you?"

She told, "Don't worry about it. I can handle it."

He said, "I know you can, but that's what I'm here for to protect and serve my lady."

Angel said, "Excuse me; I didn't know you were my man."

"Well, sweetness, you know now. So what's up?"

Angel was smiling from ear to ear that St. Louis chose her.

Angel was happy being St. Louis's woman, but she had to tell her friends Abby and Gabriel what was going on. She had been missing in action for a while, so her girls needed to know what she been up to. She called them to meet her at her apartment ASAP, so they rolled up to Angel's apartment at ten thirty, and she had breakfast ready, and they sat down and ate and discussed what Angel had been up to. Angel told her two best friends that she finally locked down St. Louis. They both were shocked because wasn't this the man they went to rob? What in the world was she thinking! Or did she fall and hit her damn head?

Angel had to break down and tell them she had feelings for him even though just a week ago they were going to rob the man.

Abby looked at Gabriel and said, "Our girl has lost her mind. Do you know what the man will do if he ever found out we were in his crib only two seconds from robbing him when he returned back home early?"

Gabriel said, "Angel sweetheart, do you know the power this man has? He could kill us, bury our assess, and no one would even miss us. Angel, what are you thinking? Are you in your feelings so deep that you don't see he using you, girl?"

Angel got so disappointed in her girls about the way they felt about her newfound relationship that she told them to get out of her house. They were pissed that Angel flipped out on them. She was changing, and it wasn't for the best. She was going loco, and they were feeling threatened by Angel for real. Angel also told her girls they can go back home as far as she was concerned. She didn't need them around anymore.

What Angel didn't know was that St. Louis found out who the culprit was that slapped her even though she didn't tell him. He took it upon himself to find out who put that hand mark on his woman's beautiful face. When he found out it was her brother, he still didn't give a damn. He wanted revenge, and he was going to have it. So St. Louis had his right-hand man set up shop outside of the restaurant that David and Dante owned so he could have a conversation with both the brothers about Angel's well-being, and if they didn't want to talk, they could settle the score with exchanging gunfire if they wanted to get down and dirty because no one was going to touch Angel as long as he was her man family member or not.

That same night, Angel ran into Gabriel and Mike coming out of the movies all hugged up and kissing. She was shocked to see her girl hugged up with her ex-man, so she walked up on them and asked Gabriel, "What the hell are you doing?"

She told Angel, "Me and Mike have been together for a while."

Angel said, "Oh, snap! So, Mike, did you tell Gabriel that me and you had being kicking for while too?"

Mike didn't know what to do, but he knew one day this would come back to bite him in the ass. Mike knew the situation was going to get even worse once Abby finds out, so Mike thought it would be best to put the shit on the table right then and there.

Mike told Angel and Gabriel that he had been seeing all three of them at different times on the low. Because all of them were very beautiful, he wanted to try out the flavor of the month, and they all tasted real sweet to him. Before he could say another word, Angel shot Mike in the chest.

When he fell down to the ground, she spit in his face and said, "I hope your punk-ass die bastard like the dog you are."

She looked up at Gabriel standing there in shell shock. Angel said. "Snap out of it, bitch, and you better be gone by daylight tomorrow or I'm going to smoke your ass too for being so trifling."

The same night, Angel and Gabriel called Abby, but neither of them got an answer, so Angel left a message telling Abby she knew about her little fling with Mike, and if she valued her life, she better be on the first thing smoking, or she would be in the hospital lying beside Mike, fighting for his life. That's all, Abby had to hear, but she wasn't taking any chances. She got her shit and got the hell out of dodge, because she knew when Angel got pissed, she would kill her own mother, so she knew she had to put some whole lot of distance between them.

That was the end of the friendship Angel had with her girls until later on down the road she had to break down and go to them for help because she was caught up between a rock and a hard spot for real.

Chapter Ten
Uprooting the Devil

ANGEL HAD BEEN spending so much time with St. Louis she had started slacking up on her grind, so she told St. Louis, "I love being with you, baby, but I have to go back to work."

He was happy to see Angel knew her priorities, so he didn't fight her on her leaving him for today. He liked a woman who got down on her grind, so he welcomed it. Angel got up the next morning, after leaving St. Louis's, and went straight to her dope house only to find out she had been ripped off for a hundred thousand dollars by one of her female soldiers, and she wanted to make an example out of her.

So she had her soldier Shaky to bring Gallia to her office. Angel took Gallia by her hair and pulled her to the floor. Angel took her forty-five out and stuck it in her mouth and said, "I'm going to ask you one time, bitch, where is my money?"

Gallia was so scared she pissed on herself. She told Angel, "I'm sorry. I'll pay you back. I promise my kids needed some things and I had to pay my rent."

Angel said, "Bitch, I don't give a flying fuck because I pay you a thousand dollars a week. You had no reason at all to steal from me."

Angel took Gallia out in the main lobby so all the soldiers could see what happens when you steal from Angel Salvador. When Angel made it out in the lobby, she had Gallia with tape wrapped around her neck with the forty-five against her temple and blew Gallia's brains out in front of everybody. It scared a lot of her soldiers except the men because they knew she was a heartless bitch, so they didn't even jump.

Gallia wasn't even a memory around there anymore, and they knew not to even speak her name until one day Gallia didn't report home and her mother got worried because her daughter always checked up on her children. She knew something bad had happened to her, so her mother went by the compound to check to see if she seen her standing on guard duty that day and she didn't, so she asked one of the female soldiers by the name of Keys have she seen Gallia, and she said, "No, not today, but if I see her, I'll tell her you stopped by."

Keys knew that Gallia's mother would never see her daughter alive again because she was floating in the bottom of the river. Keys could only wish she had someone to come and check on her because she knew it was only a matter of time before Angel turned on her. Two days passed before Angel saw St. Louis; she spoke to him every day, but they haven't spent any time together, so she called St. Louis to see if she could come by and hang out, and of course he said yes.

When she arrived at St. Louis's house, he was waiting with open arms. When she walked in the door, he had a label designer there to size Angel up. He was going to a wedding, and he wanted Angel to accompany him as his date. She was happy her man was taking her out in the open as his woman because they always stayed hiding in his house. They have only been out once as a couple, so this wedding would be nice. Angel was having fun at the wedding until someone snatched her arm and said, "What the hell are you doing here with this nigger?"

Angel turned around to see it was Dante in rear form. He was so mad he was foaming at the mouth like a pit bull.

Angel said, "Brother man, if you don't turn my arm a loose, I'm going to drop you where you stand."

Before Angel could reach for her purse all hell broke loose. St. Louis's bodyguards and Dante's right-hand man went to throwing blows like crazy, and the next thing you know, all of Dante's undercover officers were shooting. The wedding people were dropping like flies. St. Louis even got hit once in the shoulder, but he was fine.

Angel told St. Louis she was so sorry for her brother destroying his best friend wedding; she also told St. Louis she could make it up to him when they got back to his house. He smiled at her because he knew she meant every word. When Angel and St. Louis made it back to his place, he had already put a call in for the doctor to meet him at his spot to take the bullet out of his shoulder.

That night is when St. Louis decided it was time to wake Angel up from all this madness she's going through. He wanted her to see for herself that the Salvador family was dangerous to her health, and he wanted her to know they were the reason for the death of both her parents and also of her kidnapping, and David and Dante were her brothers from a different mother, and she was born in Chicago and kidnapped when she was five years old by Mr. Salvador's right-hand man Killer.

St. Louis started telling Angel what he knew about her so-called mafia family. He also had documents to back up every word. He was saying he had pictures of Cane the Hawaiian kingpin and Gloria Black her mother that she couldn't remember until the therapist she was seeing made some of her thoughts resurface. He also told Angel that her mother owned Club Sexy before she got murdered and her father Cane used to call her Baby Girl.

Angel said, "Hold up, St. Louis, this is too much information at once. Give me a minute, I need to think. If you know all this, what happened to my father the kingpin?"

He said, "Baby, your supposed-to-be grandfather Mr. Salvador and his bodyguards, including Killer, had your father to come to Hawaii to spend some time with their family and killed him in the house you were raised in."

Angel cried so hard until her nose started to bleed; she was just that angry.

Angel looked at St. Louis and she said, "Everybody that has the Salvador name is going to die, that include my brothers and that lying ass bitch Rakia a.k.a. Mommy Dearest. She is going to wish she never met Angel Carter. Thanks for telling me who I really am. St. Louis, I always felt out of place living in that family. Now I know why. I was born to Gloria Black, not to Rakia Salvador. She never mistreated me, but I never had that mother-and-daughter love that comes a long when you give birth to a child."

Angel was on a mission to get revenge on the Salvador family. She wanted them so bad that she could taste blood like a piranha; she decided to call her grandfather to come home to visit for a few days while she was there. She had plans to wipe everyone in the house out the two days she was there. Angel had called the airlines to book her departure date for that Saturday. She also called St. Louis to let him know she was going home for a few days so he wouldn't worry, but St. Louis knew something was up because Angel didn't have that sweet and sexy voice she had whenever she spoke with him.

Angel was on her way to Hawaii the next day. Killer was going to be there to pick her up when her plane lands. She was just hoping she could keep a straight face. She wanted to kill them for what they did to her parents and her. This was going to be a killing that the world would talk about for years to come. When Angel's plane landed in six hours, Killer was already there at the drop-off point waiting to see Angel. They had a big dinner plan for their little princess, but what they didn't know was their little princess was there only on a killing mission; it wasn't nothing social but all personal.

When Angel made it to the Salvador family, they greeted her with kisses and hugs. Rakia held Angel like she was her newborn baby, and Angel hated every minute of it; Angel couldn't wait until bedtime because she had mapped out her plan of destruction while she was on the plane. The family had drinks after dinner by poolside. After that, they headed to the movie room where it was set up like a real picture show. Her grandfather left everyone there to go to his office in the back of the house.

Angel thought this was the best time to go have a talk with her grandfather. She had already spiked his drink. *He should have been nodding out by now*, she thought. When Angel made it back to her grandfather's office, he was nodding so hard he didn't even notice that Angel was going through his wall safe taking all the money and information she needed on what happened to her parents. Mr. Salvador was really a sick man; he had just found out he had lung cancer, and he had been given two more months to live, and he didn't want the family to know.

Angel tied her grandfather to a chair and slapped him to wake him up. When she did, she said, "Wake up, I have to ask you a couple of questions, old man, before I kill you."

As Angel was asking her grandfather questions, her memory as a child started coming back to her: she remembered Killer and the other bodyguards talking one day in the den about how they killed Cane and how they let the pit bulls eat off his family jewels and how they made him die a slow and suffering death.

So Angel kept her mind on track and started telling her grandfather that she knew he was the one who put the hit out on her parents, and she knew he wasn't her real grandfather and that bitch of a daughter of his wasn't her real mother, and she knew Killer helped to kill her mother and kidnap her as a child. Mr. Salvador looked shocked, but he couldn't even call out for help. Angel had two needles ready that she was going to use on Mr. Salvador. But first, she wanted to cut his balls off like he did to her father; she wanted him to feel the same pain.

After Angel cut off her grandfather's family jewels, he passed out cold. She stuck the two needles she had filled with battery acid into his neck. It was a done deal. Mr. Salvador was gone without a wakeup call. Angel's next move was to go to Rakia's bedroom and hit her in the face with a hammer like Tony did to her mother, but she thought that would be too easy, so she said, *No, I want to leave Mommy Dearest for last*, so Angel proceeded down the hall to the movie room where Killer and the other bodyguards were asleep from the spiced out drinks she gave them too.

Angel went to the utility closet to collect some rope. She tied Killer and the bodyguards up, and she went out to the pool and let the water out and filled it up with acid. She took their eyeballs out with an ice pick and put them in a glass for the pit bulls to eat. After she did that, she pulled all three of them to the pool and threw them in the pool of acid. Angel knew it was time to go see Mommy Dearest; she left the best one for last.

Angel went into Rakia's bedroom, and she was asleep, so Angel didn't wake her. She took two pairs of handcuffs out her goodie bag and handcuffed Rakia to the bedpost. She went out to the garage and got the gas can that they kept out near the lawn mower. Angel rushed back in the house because she wanted to wake her up by beating the shit out of her before she let her know what she did to her by killing her parents. Angel hated Rakia so bad she whooped her ass; then she turned around, took a pair of wire pliers, and pulled each one of her teeth out why she was wide awake. When Rakia passed out, Angel took the gasoline, poured it all over Rakia, lit a cigarette, thumped it on Rakia, and set her on fire.

After the house went up in flames, Angel proceeded to go out into the yard to kill both of the pit bulls. They were jumping around the yard, barking. Angel took her thirty-eight and blew both their brains out. Angel stood down the street with the rest of the people that was watching the fire. No one noticed her because she was dressed in a disguise.

They next day, she was back on a plane headed back to Chicago, and St. Louis was hot on her trail. He had followed her to Hawaii without her knowing. He just went as backup if she needed him. He was only going to be a phone call away. When Angel touched down in Chicago, St. Louis was the first person she called. She wanted to release a little stress. She had finally got rid of some of the Salvador family. She still had her brothers to deal with, and their time was coming to a close very soon.

St. Louis made it to Angel's place real quick. She wrapped her arms around him and kissed him long and hard. He knew she had blood all over her hands, so he knew she needed a relief and was there for the taking. They made love all night. When they woke up the next morning, St. Louis asked her did she want to talk about anything.

She said, "No, not right now, but I do want to talk about taking my brothers off this earth. If you want to talk about that, I'm all ears."

Angel put plans in order to protect her brothers' properties; she want to take over all of their businesses before she killed them, but she had to put up a front with them like she changed, and to get on their good side, she invited them over to lunch, and they both accepted because they wanted their little sister back. So Angel played the little sister's role very well, and they both fell for her act.

While Dante and David were sitting there having lunch with Angel, they received a phone call from a mafia kingpin by the name of Caruso. He told them their whole family had been killed and they need to return home as soon as possible to make the funeral arrangements for their family, and they needed to find out who would be so bold to wipe out a whole mafia family in one night. Dante, David, and Angel were on the first plane on their way home, and when they arrived, it wasn't a home to go home to, but of course Angel knew she killed every one, including the dogs.

Dante was heated because they didn't even have bodies to even bury. They had to meet with the family lawyer for the will reading Mr. Salvador had left everything too all three grandchildren. They had twenty million dollars to split up between the three of them. When they heard the will reading of the money and the overseas account of a billion dollars, they almost choked, but they kept their composure.

After they got their checks from the lawyer, it was time for them to bounce, and they headed back to Chicago to come up with a plan to find out what happened to their family, even though Angel faked the crying part to convince her brothers that she was feeling the pain behind the death of their loved ones. If Dante and David really knew, she would be dead.

David and Dante were on a rampage ever since the death of their family. They were so bitter until they started blackmailing the clients and didn't care who they hurt in the process. Dante got drunk one night driving around the city and hit an innocent bystander crossing the street and killed him, and he didn't even stop to see if the person was dead.

The next day, Angel started her plan to take her brothers out of their misery. She knew they had her wills too, but she didn't care if they left her anything because she had enough money to burn. She asked her brothers to meet her at Club Sexy that night.

Angel knew just how to get her brothers to meet her at Club Sexy. She told them that she found out who killed their family, and that she would be sitting in her car waiting on their arrival. When David and Dante pulled up, they saw Angel's car, and they went over to Angel's car and got in. When Dante got in the back seat and David got in the back, it didn't really matter at this point because both of them had to die.

Angel started off by saying, "Did you two know that our grandfather ordered a hit on our father, and that he had his eyeballs cut out and feed them to the pit bulls?"

Dante and David said, "Yes, we were there to see it happen." But they both wanted to know how she found out. They also told Angel her crackhead ass mother was a home wrecker and she got dealt with too.

Angel was so pissed she started shooting inside her car. She forgot St. Louis was in her trunk. She put so many holes in her brothers that they both looked like swiss cheese. She drove out of the parking lot fast as she could and then got two blocks from the club and jumped out of her car and popped the trunk. When she saw St. Louis's eyes open and wasn't hurt, she jumped for joy.

St. Louis and Angel drove her car to a secluded area and took the plates off her car and set the car on fire. Two days later, the police found Angel's car after she reported her brothers missing. She also told them that David borrowed her car the early part of the day so it won't put suspicion on her.

The police told Angel that they were burned up so bad until she wouldn't even have to have a funeral for her brothers, but they will keep the case open until they find out who murdered her brothers.

Chapter Eleven
Who is Mike Trivet?

MIKE HAD FINALLY gotten out of the hospital, but before he got released, he had an envelope delivered to him by a mail carrier; this was sent by Mr. Salvador before his demise, and it was only to be delivered by his attorney if anything was to happen to him. Mike didn't know who this Mr. Salvador person was, but he found out when he opened the envelope it was an explanation from Mr. Salvador telling Mike that he's sorry for the family giving him up for adoption.

Mike was Cane's son born to Mr. Salvador's maid. He found out that Cane was having an affair with his maid Rosa. He was so pissed that Cane had no respect for his daughter that he kept Rosa on as the maid until she gave birth, and once she gave birth to a seven-pound-six-ounce boy, he made Rosa put the baby up for adoption and she was to never speak of a having a baby again unless she wanted to end up dead.

Cane never knew she had his child. He knew something was up because he got sent to Chicago to run the family business. Mr. Salvador knew who adopted the baby; he kept up with his upbringing, and he also sent money to his grandmother when his adoption mother died.

He also had pictures of every football game he was in, and he sent the pictures alone with the money he sent in the envelope that got sent to the hospital. Mr. Salvador also had pictures of Angel and David and Dante.

"These are your brothers. Angel, this pretty little princess, is your sister by your father. All of you were born to different mothers, and I hope you can forgive me for taking your family away from you.

"If you are reading this letter, that means I have moved on and just maybe you can start a relationship with your brothers and sister."

Mike was shell-shocked because he had not only slept with his sister but his sister shot him and left him for dead. How could he tell her that all the times that they were saying he looked familiar that in reality he was their brother, by a different mother? He knew he wouldn't be forgiven from Angel, but he thought he would be able to get it from Dante and David.

While Mike was trying to get his thoughts together, he saw the breaking news on the TV coming with a report of Angel's car and the two bodies that they found in the car. The first thing Mike thought about was Angel. He said, *Angel had her name all over his brothers' death*. Mike had to get out of that hospital quick because he knew from Abby, still staying in touch with him, that the whole Salvador family had be killed, including the dogs, and if Angel did that, he knew she would be after him next.

What Mike didn't know was Angel had copies of every letter Mr. Salvador sent to Mike. She knew Mike was her brother, and she also knew Tony was her brother too, and so were Dante and David. She also found out that Cane has a daughter out there somewhere too through the documents from Salvador's safe. She was born the same time Angel was. Cane's other daughter's mother was a social service worker in the Chicago area, so Angel is on top of finding her also.

In the documents that Angel took out of Mr. Salvador's safe had Cane's other daughter's mother name written down on paper: her name was Helen Davis. Once she goes down to the social service department and find Helen Davis, she would find her sister, but she didn't want Mike around, period. She wanted him dead also, but Mike was smarter than his twin brothers. He wanted Angel dead that way he could build an empire of his own. Mike got out of the hospital and went to stay in hotel away from the city. He didn't want to be spotted by any of Angel's soldiers.

Mike had his mind made up he had to come up with a master plan if he wanted Angel. He couldn't even go back to his office because he knew Angel probably had his home and his job on lockdown. Angel had her soldiers all over the Chicago area looking for Mike. Angel knew he was released from the hospital; her soldiers didn't get to the hospital on time to get Mike as he left the hospital early.

The next day, Mike went and borrowed a car from a buddy of his so he could go scope out Angel's apartment. Mike wanted to catch Angel by herself, but little did he know she was wrapped around St. Louis like a python, so mike thought that he would disguise himself like an old man and go hang out in Angel's club. He wanted to hook up with one of Angel's strippers. That way he could get one step closer to Angel.

Mike was sitting in Angel's club one night when Angel and St. Louis walked in. Mike said to himself, *Look at her, looking like a million bucks knowing she's deranged as hell that bitch wipe out a whole mafia family. I'm going to see to it that bitch pay for killing our brothers if that's the last thing I do.*

Angel and St. Louis were beginning to be a very hot couple. They spent a lot of time together. That's why Mike couldn't catch her alone just of yet. Mike followed Angel and St. Louis from the club that night. They went back to St. Louis's house, and when Mike saw that, he thought, *I can kill two birds with one stone*, but in reality, Mike didn't like St. Louis because for real St. Louis reminded Mike too much of himself.

Mike didn't know his adoptive mother had a son when she was sixteen and put him up for adoption before her mother found out she was pregnant. She and her boyfriend went to some bootleg doctor when she went into labor, and it scared her from ever having children of her own. That's why she adopted Mike. Of course, St. Louis reminded him of himself because they are brothers with the same father.

Mike watched St. Louis's house all night, but he knew it wasn't going to be easy trying to get to Angel as long as she was guarded by St. Louis. So Mike decided to wait and come up with a better approach. He wanted Angel so bad because she shot him, and now to find out she's his sister to man; this is too much, and to get a call from Gabriel telling him she's having my daughter is so unreal. Mike always wanted a little princess, so now he would have one in six months.

Mike wanted to be around for the birth of his daughter so he had to make sure Angel was buried six feet deep. What Mike didn't know was that Angel knew his every move since the day he left the hospital. Her soldiers got there too late, but she and St. Louis was there on time. They both knew how Mike tried to disguise himself, and they know he followed them to St. Louis's house. Angel and St. Louis were setting the trap for Mike to fall right into Angel's hand.

Angel is having a celebration party for the new business she just opened up; it's another club she calls it Sexy Sophistication. Even to enter Angel's new club, Sexy Sophistication, you have to be dressed to impress. She even had a cover charge of fifty dollars, and after ten, the cover charge is sixty dollars. Mike was going to the celebration, and he was going to be prepared for whatever, but what Mike didn't know the night of the opening of Club Sophistication he wasn't even going to make it out of his hotel room. St. Louis had his right-hand man on guard at the Ritz Hotel, where Mike was staying. He should have had since enough to check in to a dump.

Mike was in the shower when St. Louis's right-hand man snuck into Mike's room. He had some guitar wire that he was going to tie Mike up with until Angel got there, and Angel's plan was to go show her face in Club Sexy Sophistication and sneak out long enough to go kill Mike and get back before anyone notice she was gone. When Angel made it to the hotel, Mike was sitting in a chair tied up and bleeding. Angel looked at Mike and said, "Oh, what a tangle web we weave!"

Mike said to Angel, "Bitch, you can kill me, but I will meet you in hell one day for sure."

Angel took that guitar wire and wrapped it around Mike's penis until it snapped off. Mike bled so much his eyes rolled around in his head. Angel looked at Mike and said, "Don't pass out now, brother dear. I'm not finished yet."

What Angel did next made Mike pass out for real. She had St. Louis's right-hand man screw Mike pretty ass in the ass.

After that little session was over, Angel took a machete and cut Mike's head off, and they took the rest of Mike's body and put it in a plastic bag and had it delivered to the police station. When the officer at the front desk found the bag by his desk, he opened it up and threw up all over the police station; it was horrifying. The whole squad was on a mission to find out who would be so bold to kill Chicago's prominent attorney Mike Trivet.

The case of Mike Trivet was all over the news worldwide. Posters of his face were plastered all over the news. When Angel got up that morning, the news was on, and she saw Mike's face and got angry all over again. She even spit on her own television screen. Angel said to herself, *I should have had him burned alive just for disrespecting me and my friends.*

When Gabriel saw the news, she started having pains in her abdomen. She couldn't believe what she was seeing. She had just talked to Mike an hour ago about their daughter and baby names, and for some reason this didn't sit well with Gabriel. She knew Angel had something to do with the death of her unborn child's father, and she also knew that Angel took out her own mafia family, the Salvadors. Gabriel knew her father was head of a mafia organization too and needed to go home to Hawaii to speak with her father. Someone had to stop Angel by any means necessary. Angel had turned into the devil himself and needed to be stopped.

Gabriel made it home just in time; her father was getting ready to leave for a trip, but Gabriel wanted him to know that his best friend Mr. Salvador was killed by Angel, and she also killed Dante and David, and the father of her unborn child. Gabriel's father was speechless; he wanted to know why she thought that Angel was responsible for the death of her own family.

Gabriel told her father that Mike had just found out that the Salvadors really weren't Angel's biological family and that Cane was her father and that Mr. Salvador was the one who ordered the hit on both of her parents. Gabriel told her father that Angel threatened to kill her also because they were both seeing the same guy. Gabriel also told her father that Angel threatened Abby as well.

Gabriel's father told her not to worry because he was going to put some people on to Angel's. He had some Russian hit men that owed him a favor, and they would love to set fire to Angel's ass. Gabriel's father called in his favor before he left for his trip, and they were glad to go after some fresh meat. Angel was happy being alone in the world without family until she met St. Louis and moved into his place so he could keep an eye on her.

What St. Louis didn't know is when the Russians came looking for her, they would kill everyone in her house to get to the people they want. Gabriel had given her father all the information he needed to get to Angel, including her clubs and all six buildings she was now running. The Russians set up camp in Chicago, and they even rented a black Tahoe with Chicago plates so they wouldn't looked suspects.

The Russians were there to commit a path of destruction. Angel was going to pay one way or the other. Gabriel wanted to pay for killing her unborn child's father, and Gabriel hated Angel. She even thought about being her friend again just to get close enough to her to cut her throat. Angel had forgotten all about her friends, Gabriel and Abby. They were best friends once; now they were on Angel's shit list, and Angel was a devise, conniving killing machine bitch. She was not to be trusted. They wanted Angel dead so the both of them could move on.

Chapter Twelve
The Russian Mafia

The Russians looked for Angel like she told them; they had money and pictures of Angel from Gabriel's father. The Russian mafia was like no other family: when they come for you, they wanted blood. Gabriel was hoping to hear some news soon about Angel's demise; she really wanted Angel to suffer because Gabriel was about to become a single parent, and she didn't know how she was going to be able to raise her daughter on her own. The Russians were sitting outside Angel's club and her apartment buildings.

The Russians even had St. Louis's house watched as well. St. Louis knew something wasn't right because this black Tahoe would show up on different days parked down the street, so he let Angel know that they are being watched by some very powerful people and was going to call in some favors. St. Louis knew that the Russians didn't play. He didn't want Angel worrying about it too much right now because they just found out that she maybe pregnant.

St. Louis called a couple people he knew that could find out who these guys could be. When St. Louis got the call back saying that Gabriel's father put a Russian hit out on Angel's, St. Louis knew that he had to come up with a plan to get Angel out of town for a while. He also knew it wasn't going to be easy trying to get past the Russians.

The Russians had three trucks watching each spot, so St. Louis knew he had to come up with a plan quick. When St. Louis started telling Angel he wanted her to take a trip alone, she knew then that he was trying to save her from the Russians. Angel came up with a plan of her own: if they wanted her, they had to bring it. So Angel told St. Louis, "With your soldiers and mine, we could bring Iraqi to Chicago, and them Russians wouldn't know what hit them."

Angel and St. Louis rounded up their soldiers for a meeting. They were going to take this killing to a whole other level, especially since the Russians came on their turf. Angel had to go back to the gun shop where she knew this guy called Dakota. She knew he had it bad for her, and she could get him to do just about anything for her, so she had to use Dakota to her advances. Angel called Dakota to see if he was at work because she didn't have time to waste. He told Angel he was at work, and to stop by and see him, Angel took Dakota up on his offer, and thirty minutes later, Angel was walking through the door.

Angel had a truck parked in the alley behind the gun store. She told Dakota she had fifty thousand dollars to spend for artillery and she wanted everything, from missiles to hand grenades. She wanted those Russians to never think about coming on anyone's turf again without thinking because you have to bring ass to get ass, and Angel was going to take as much ass as they brought.

That night, the Russians had plans in striking Angel in her apartment. They were going to blow up all her properties to make her come out in the open. What the Russians didn't know was Angel and St. Louis had a army of soldiers that was ready for war; they were camped outside down the street from where the Russians had their Tahoe parked. One of Angel's soldiers name Eastside was ready with a missile in a van parked right behind the Russians Tahoe. They weren't going to make it back to their vehicles at all. They were going to die like Denzel Washington did in *Training Day*, but their demise was going to be far worst. When the Russians stepped out their vehicles to walk up to Angel's apartment building, armed with machine guns, they had no idea that Angel's and St. Louis's army of soldiers were going to attack from all corners of Angel's whole block. They lit them, Russian men, up like a Christmas tree on Christmas. It was so loud on Angel's block that they didn't even hear the police sirens coming from afar. By the time Angel's soldiers realized the police was on the set, they turned around and started blowing up the police cars with the hand grenades. The Russians that were sent to kill Angel couldn't even go home in body bags; the artillery that Angel got from Dakota ripped through them Russians like they were chopped beef in a supermarket.

Angel and St. Louis had enough soldiers to kill at least four states of people, but they also lost twenty people that night, but they could be replaced. It was like a bad nightmare; when the other police arrived on the scene, the news reporters were all over the scene. What people watched that night made them scared to live in the Windy City. The people knew Chicago was just like any other town as far as the drug game goes, but the killings had the people of Chicago in an uproar. They wanted Angel and all the other drug dealers like St. Louis to be ran out of their town.

Gabriel's father had seen the news and was shocked to see Angel had that kind of power to kill off the Russians that he sent to kill her. Mr. Dane knew Mr. Salvador; taught Angel's survival skills, well, she could hear a mice crawl across a floor on cotton. Mr. Dane knew he had to straighten this mess out because by him sending the Russians after Angel, he was the reason they were dead, and he knew that now his family was in danger the Russian mafia now had him and his family on a hit list, so he had to get his family somewhere safe.

What Mr. Dane didn't know was St. Louis had already paid off the Russian mafia family to leave him and Angel alone since the killing spree in the middle of street. So those coming at them sideways again would be dangerous for their health because their army was as big as the Russians. The thing with St. Louis was he wasn't about to get played by no punk-ass Russian mafia because as far as St. Louis was concerned, he was the mafia kingpin of Chicago and no one was going to chase him away from his city.

Two days later, Mr. Dane had his family moved; he had ten of his best bodyguards to take his family to one of his safe houses in Montana, where they could be safe; he told his wife that he would be close behind them in a couple days once his family was gone. Mr. Dane called Boris, the head of the Russian mafia, to try and set up a meeting. Boris agreed to the meeting because two of the Russian guys that got killed by Angel and her soldiers were two of Boris's sons.

Mr. Boris wanted someone's head for the loss of his two sons. He wanted to know what favor that his sons owe Mr. Dane because he should have talked to him before he sent his sons on a mission to kill someone in Chicago. Mr. Dane met Mr. Boris at a restaurant where he was having dinner with his wife Isabella. She was so upset about her sons' death she couldn't stop crying, and Mr. Boris wanted Mr. Dane to see the pain in her eyes. Mr. Dane looked at Isabella with hurt in his heart. He didn't know Angel was that deranged, but he knew she was a trained killer.

Mr. Dane talked with Mr. Boris and told that he was sorry for his loss. He also told Mr. Boris that his two sons owe him a favor because one night when they were out drunk, they raped a sixteen-year-old young lady who was walking home from a party, since they didn't want Mr. Boris to know what they did, they went to Mr. Dane to clean up their mess.

Mr. Boris knew what Mr. Dane did for his sons; he would always appreciate his help, but now his sons were dead because some half-breed bitch decided to take their lives, he wanted to know where Angel lived, because this time around she was going to feel what it was like to suffer the loss of a child.

Mr. Boris looked at Mr. Dane and said, "You have two children yourself, don't you?"

Mr. Dane said, "Yes."

He didn't know why he asked him that question, but what came out Mr. Boris's mouth next made Mr. Dane reach over the table and punch Mr. Boris in the mouth.

Mr. Boris told Mr. Dane, "I have killed your bodyguards and will have your wife and daughters under protective custody until you kill Angel. After the job is done, you can have your family back in one piece. If you don't bring me the head of Angel Carter, the heads of your wife and daughters would be delivered to you in a hat box. Do you understand?"

Mr. Dane was pissed; he agreed to go kill Angel personally because he felt he could get close to her because his daughter and Angel grew up together.

Mr. Dane was on a suicide mission; he was going to kill Angel, and he didn't want anything to happen to his family; he took ten of his personal bodyguards with him to Chicago. He knew Angel had her own personal army, so he had to think of a plan to get Angel to meet him alone. St. Louis wasn't letting Angel go to the restroom by herself, so he trying to get Angel alone wasn't going to happen.

Mr. Dane made it to Chicago three days. Later on the fourth day, he gave Angel a call letting her know he was in town and wanted to see her. She agreed to meet with him but at a secluded area on her turf. He wasn't expecting for Angel to be so harsh with him, but Angel wasn't taking any chances with her life anymore, so she had to be very cautious, plus St. Louis wasn't letting Angel go nowhere without him being by her side. Mr. Dane made it to the spot in record time but was disappointed that Angel had her guards at the door to search him and his two bodyguards.

Angel had it set up in her mind that he was there for a reason, and she was definitely going to find out because all of a sudden these crime families were coming after her, so she knew he was coming next, so she wanted to hear what he had to say. Angel knew if he said anything to her about her fake ass mafia crime family—the Salvadors, she was going to split his wig wide open.

Mr. Dane started by asking, "Angel, how are you doing?"

She said, "I've been fine. Now I know you didn't come all the way to Chicago to see if I was fine. Why didn't you come to see how I was doing when my family got killed?" He lied and told Angel he was out of town on business when that went down with her family; he also told Angel he was sorry for her loss, and he was there now.

Angel was feeling like there was something on Mr. Dane's mind, but she held her thoughts. She wanted him to speak now or forever hold his peace, because when it was all said and done, she had the last word. So Mr. Dane asked Angel had she seen Gabriel just to clear the air a little. He told her that her mother spoke with her and they found out that they were going to be grandparents. What he had just said to Angel made the hair stand up on the back of her neck. She said to herself, *Oh, so Gabriel is pregnant by Mike. That hoe won't have that baby not if I have anything to do with it.*

Angel was getting disgusted looking at Mr. Dane. She wanted to know why he was really there; Angel started getting a little uneasy, so she decided to put the shit on the table.

"Mr. Dane, I know you are the one who put the Russian guys up to come here to Chicago to kill me."

When she said that, Mr. Dane's eyeglasses fell down from his eyes to his nose. He stepped back to get a good look at Angel to see if she was joking.

Angel snapped her fingers and out came St. Louis from the back, walking an alligator. He had him trained to eat at a blink of an eye in order to prove he had the alligator trained on point. He told the alligator to go stand over there by Mr. Dane, so St. Louis said, "Mr. Dane, I'm going to ask you one time why you are here, and if you lie to me or to my woman, my alligator Ralph is going to eat your bodyguards one by one."

Mr. Dane started to look at St. Louis like he was crazy. "I don't give a damn about my bodyguards. They get paid to work for me. Their life is to protect me by all means necessary."

Before Mr. Dane could say another word, his bodyguard Tommy started talking like he had verbal diarrhea. He didn't want to become alligator's food, so he looked at Angel with fear in his eyes, almost begging for his life. He knew if they made it out of there, he was going to die by Mr. Dane's hands either way.

Angel had seen enough. She wanted the alligator to have his dinner, so she told St. Louis to fuck the small talk and get down to business because she had a doctor's appointment she didn't want to miss. After the alligator had his dinner—the two bodyguards, Mr. Dane was next, and he wasn't afraid to die.

He told Angel, "When you kill me, you still won't be safe, because it's more crime families like me that want you dead, bitch, so you better watch your back because they won't stop until they put your ass in the dirt."

Angel went face-to-face with Mr. Dane, and she spit in his face and said, "I'm going to kill your whole family, especially your pregnant ass daughter so you can go straight to hell. Maybe, one day I'll see you there."

Chapter Thirteen
Amy Leaving Chicago

WHEN AMY FOUND out for sure that Angel had kidnapped her son Conner, she knew she had to leave town, but she was in love with Angel's brother David. She didn't want to leave David. He brought her son back to her, and she would be forever thankful to him for that, but at the time David didn't want to leave his sister and brother, they came to Chicago together to make money, but once David and Dante found out that Angel was a loose cannon, they needed to separate themselves from her, but they had no idea that Angel had plan to put them to sleep permanently.

Angel was on her way to check in on her club when she spotted a girl who looked just like Amy and that struck a light in Angel. Now that David was dead, she can get back on course with kidnapping Amy's son Conner. She had so much animosity build up for Amy because if she had not been in a relationship with her brother, they would have never known about her black market baby-selling enterprise. Angel said to herself, *Once I leave my club, I'm going by Amy's apartment to see what I can see if she's still staying there.* When Angel made it on Amy's street, she was hit by disappointment because Amy's apartment was empty. She had moved on. Angel didn't know where, but she knew she was going to have her found.

Amy knew it wouldn't be long before Angel came looking for her as soon as she crossed her mind again. She had to get her baby boy away from harm. She hadn't talked to her mother for four years, and she thought it was time to make an appearance. She prayed everything will go smooth when she made it home to Montana to visit her mother and introduce her to her grandson Conner. While Angel was over at Amy's apartment looking for her, Amy was on a redeye, headed to Montana to see her mother.

When Amy made it to her mother's house in Montana, she was scared to knock on her door, but when the door swung open, Amy was shocked to see her mother standing there with open arms. She was so happy to see her. She thought for years that her daughter was dead she hired private investigators that couldn't find Amy, and for Amy to show up four years later without even a letter or postcard, it was what her mother prayed for a chance to be united with her daughter again. What Amy's mother didn't know was Amy really wasn't there for herself, but she was there to make sure her son couldn't be found by Angel.

Angel had to find out where Amy was, and she knew she had to give Mr. Hayes a call and put him on retainer again to find Amy and her son. Angel gave Mr. Hayes the pictures of Amy and her son, but she knew nothing about Amy to give him the information he needed to find Amy but as long as he tried was all she needed.

Amy told her mother where she been and what she was doing for the last four years, and she also told her mom about Angel and how she had her son kidnapped. Her mother was in awe because she couldn't believe that her daughter had been through so much turmoil at such a young age. She mostly blamed herself because if she was home enough, Amy never would have gotten molested by her stepfather. Her mother worked so much that she didn't stop to recognize she had a young daughter who needed her mother to teach her how to become a woman.

Amy told her mother that she forgave her for her shortcomings and just wanted the two of them to move forward. Her mother waited four years to hear her daughter say that, and it made her feel real warm inside; she had forgiveness from God. Now she had it from her daughter and she now had peace, but Amy's mother wanted to know who Conner's father was because he could keep Conner safe and away from Angel. Amy told her mother that Conner's father name was Ronald Louis. They had sex once, and she never told him about Conner. He doesn't even know the he has a son.

Ronald Louis a.k.a. St. Louis didn't know he had a son because he was the kind of guy to hit it and quit it back in the day. It would be a dark day if he knew Conner even existed because he wanted children but never knew who his parents were, and he was going to make sure he would be the perfect father. Part of this situation would be from him finding out that Angel kidnapped his son once and she wanted his mother dead. That would be one hell of an altercation because it would be a choice he would have to make between the love he has for his woman or the chance to be the perfect father to his son.

Amy's mother asked her, "Do you know how to get in contact with Mr. Ronald Louis?"

She told her mother, "Yes, he stays in Chicago, where I came from. I didn't want him to know our son because he's a drug lord. I wanted my son to live a normal life, not in the shadow of his father selling drugs."

"I understand what you saying, Amy, but your son needs his father's help in keeping him safe from that crazy, deranged woman, Angel."

"Mother, word on the street is that Ronald is dating Angel. I don't know how true it is, but her brother David that I was dating told me she was before Angel killed him."

"Angel killed her own brother?"

"Yes, she did, and she wants to kill me and kidnap my son and sell him to the highest bidder in her black market baby-selling enterprise."

"Oh, my Amy, you need to go to the police."

"I can't do that, Mother. She has so much money she has half the police department on payroll, and judges. I don't want to take that chance until my son is somewhere safe. I don't even feel safe now because Montana is still not far enough for me." Amy told her mother, "I really want to go back to Chicago to make sure I set Angel up to get busted, but I didn't know who to trust on the police force."

Amy's mother was happy her daughter was back home, but what she told her about her life scared her to death. She was afraid for her daughter and grandson. She was also scared for her own life as well, so she knew she had to come up with a plan to help Amy, so she knew a couple of people who worked underground who help women that were in danger of abusive husbands, so her mother gave them a called, and they gave her a number to call them at this pay phone they had setup for the women to call them on. Amy gave them a call, and she and Conner were rushed out the house at two thirty in the morning to a safe house.

Amy left her mother's house just in time because Mr. Hayes was hot on her trail. How he knew where to find Amy's mother was a shot in the dark, but he was good at his job. That's why Angel kept him on retainer. Mr. Hayes watched Amy's mother's house for four days and never saw any sign of Amy and Conner, so he decided to tap Amy's mother's phone to see if she would contact her by phone, but Amy couldn't call her mom. She agreed when she went underground that she couldn't contact anyone.

Angel wanted to know had Mr. Hayes contacted Amy because he had supposed to give Angel a call in two days, but Angel hadn't heard from him, so she called him to see if he had any news for her. When Mr. Hayes saw Angel number, he didn't want to answer because he didn't have any information to give her on Amy as of yet, but he answered the phone anyway just to let her know that he was in Montana and found Amy's mother but Amy wasn't around, but he was sure she would be showing up sooner or later.

Amy was miserable being underground because she didn't know anyone, but she met a woman called Robin in the program she was in. She was cool, Amy thought, but she was scared to trust anyone because she knew Angel had long arms and money, and she didn't want her to reach out and touch her without her knowing. Robin became a good friend to Amy. They shared a bedroom together with their children. They both had boys, so Conner and Eddie got along fine, so Amy and Robin got real tight like sisters, so Amy decided one night to tell Robin about her past.

Robin wasn't shocked about the things Amy was telling her because she herself was underground because her husband of ten years tried to cut her throat while she was asleep because he wanted out of their marriage without giving her a dime, plus he was taking Robin to court for custody of their son Eddie that he had been sexually abusing too since the time he was two—now Eddie was six years old, and Robin didn't want him to have her son; he was already traumatized.

Amy wanted so bad to get back at Angel that she told Robin, but Robin told her that she could find someone in the prosecuting attorney's office that could help her put a stop to Angel's behavior because she had to be stopped. Robin also told Amy that she never heard of a woman that was so heartless in her life. She even told Amy that she didn't think Angel had a soul, but Robin agreed that Amy made the right decision to bring her son underground for safety because if Angel is that dangerous, she need to stay out of her reach.

Angel had plans for Amy. Whenever Mr. Hayes came back with information on Amy, she wanted Amy to pay for running from the house the night she went into labor with Conner. Angel felt like Amy owes her for getting her off the street while she was pregnant. Angel also hated the fact that Amy was dating her brother, and Amy didn't back off like she told her to. Amy had her mind made up to go back to Chicago to put the ball in motion for Angel to get busted for all her wrongdoings, but first Amy had to ask Robin would she keep her little boy safe while she was gone because Amy was tired of running and hiding from Angel. She wanted to be able to enjoy life with her son without hiding out and watching her back.

Angel got a call from Mr. Hayes saying that Amy was a no show and that she haven't even called her mother at all so his trip was a wasted trip. He told Angel that the trip was on him because this was the first time he ever been defeated, so he hoped that Angel would still keep him on retainer, and she told him that she would.

Angel said to Mr. Hayes, "This woman is just like smoke. She disappeared without a trace, unbelievable. It's fine because one day she will show up somewhere, and when she does, Angel Carter will be waiting."

Angel's devil side kicked in while she was talking to Mr. Hayes. She thought about kidnapping Amy's mother to bring her out of hiding, so she asked Mr. Hayes what was the address to Amy's mother's house so she can send someone to pick her up to bring her to Chicago. Mr. Hayes was more than happy to give Angel the address because he was ready to leave Montana and get back to his office; he had two more cases that he was neglecting for Angel.

Amy told Robin what she had plan to do, and Robin was glad to keep Conner for her, and Amy left the next morning after breakfast and headed back to Chicago to the prosecuting attorney office. When Amy made it to Chicago, she went to the police station. She got scared soon as she saw one of the officers that worked for Angel, but he didn't see her, so she proceeded to go up to the desk and asked the officer at the desk if she could speak with the prosecutor. He told Amy to sign her name on the sign-in sheet and have a seat. Amy waited for twenty minutes before she was escorted back to the prosecutor's office. She smiled because she knew she was on her way to turn the tables on Angel Salvador a.k.a. Angel Carter.

Chapter Fourteen
Angel Getting Busted

AMY GAVE THE whole rundown on the Angel Carter's business. She told the prosecutor about the killings of Angel's brothers. She also told that Angel kidnapped her son to sell him. She told that Angel was in charge of six buildings that she owned with drugs, gambling, and black market baby-selling, and she had a room in her basement that she had set up like a hospital room for teenage girls that were pregnant, and nowhere to go, she was killing them and putting their children up for sale in her black market baby-selling enterprise.

The prosecutor wasn't by far surprised about what Amy was saying because he had been working for Angel's brothers before they got killed. He knew Angel hand her hand in just about everything that Chicago had to offer, and he also knew if he went up against Angel, he better have all his eggs in a basket. The prosecutor Mr. John Jones was up for reelection, so this would be right up his alley to bring a woman down with the status of Angel Carter. He knew somebody was running Chicago, but to hear it was a female, he wanted to meet this Angel Carter in person.

Mr. Jones put in a call to the commissioner to set up a meeting to shut Angel's businesses down and to arrest her, but he knew to get a judge to sign a warrant, he had to have more than just some she say evidence, so he decided to stake out the residents of Angel's establishments to see if he could get some pictures and see who was coming and going and what kind of people that was hanging out there. Mr. Jones watched Angel's place for two weeks. What he saw next coming out of Angel's building blew his mind; it was Judge Clinton Blake, the judge that he took his case to about Angel Carter.

Mr. Jones knew it was some shady things going on, so he wanted to get a little closer to the situation, so he wanted to see if he could get a pass to get into

Angel's strip club. He caught one of Angel's strippers coming out the club one night and propositioned her.

Mr. Jones asked her, "Did you want to make a thousand dollars?"

Stripper said, "What I got to do for you?"

He told Casey the stripper, "I just need you to get me into Club Sophistication, that's all."

She said, "Mister, for a thousand dollars I would get you a backstage pass to Halle Berry's dressing room. Give me my thousand dollars and we can go in right now."

Casey took Mr. Jones into the club, and he sat in a corner, taking pictures of everyone who was there. The judge was sitting there getting a lap dance from one of the strippers; he was pulling twenties out his pocket like he had a hole in it. He thought to himself, *I am going to blow the top off the Windy City of Chicago.* And it was going to be judges and lawyers and police officers going down. He had never seen so many city officials working for the illegal side of the law.

Mr. Jones knew he was going to have to go over the judges' head and the commissioner because he didn't know who he could trust because Angel had the city on lock. Mr. Jones went to the mayor with the pictures and voice-recorded conversations he had with undercover police officers he saw at the club that night. The officers were so high off the blow they were snorting that night that they didn't even notice Mr. Jones wasn't a part of the game plan. He was only there to bring their behind to the ground.

The next day, Mr. Jones called Amy to see if she would testify against Angel when he had her arrested. Amy was happy that they were finally going to arrest Angel. Mr. Jones wanted to put Amy in protected custody, but he didn't know how long she would be in protected custody. Amy needed to know because she didn't want to be away from her son too long, but she did want to see Angel's face once that locked her up, plus she wanted to tell St. Louis about their son. When Mr. Jones got the mayor to get a judge, he could trust to issue a warrant for Angel and her business, it was all she wrote.

Angel woke up the next morning feeling sick. She told St. Louis something was wrong and she didn't feel safe something was about to go down. She told St. Louis that she needed to move some things around.

"I want Amy's mother to be moved to our warehouse in Kansas City for now because something is not adding up, baby."

As soon as Angel moved Amy's mother, she got a call stating that all of her business had been kicked in by johnny law, and they were looking high and low for Angel. They couldn't find her because she was staying at St. Louis's house.

They didn't know about Angel and St. Louis relationship, so they had to find out from one of the undercover officers that they had in custody.

Hammer was really put into David's and Dante's fold as an informant; he had enough to send them to jail for the rest of their life. He had to pretend that he killed his own son. Hammer didn't like his son, but he wouldn't kill him for two want-to-be kingpins. He had set up a dummy look-alike for his son. It was so real that the people on the series face-off couldn't have done it better, so when Hammer brought the deal to Mr. Jones, he accepted because now he had two people to testify for the *city of Chicago v. Angel Carter.*

Angel was so nervous that the police was hot on her trail that she had to leave the Chicago area for a while just until she have her baby now she was going to be a mother for the first time, and then she would know what it feels like to have that motherly bond with your child. Angel wind up in Memphis. She stayed in hiding for four months. She had a baby girl, and she named her Gloria, after her deceased mother. Two months after the birth of her daughter, someone in Memphis saw Angel's picture on the *Most Wanted* television show, and the police kicked in the door and arrested Angel Carter.

Chapter Fifteen
Abby and Gabriel

ABBY HAD LEFT Chicago the night Angel called and threatened her about the secret relationship she was having with Mike. Abby went back home to Hawaii. She knew what was going on with Angel, killing her own family. She knew Angel was a twisted person, and when she found out on the news that Mike was dead too, she really started to shake because she was pregnant to with Mike's child. She told her mother that she was pregnant by a guy that she met at a bar which turned out to be a one-night stand. Abby's mother was so upset she turned beet red.

Abby tried calling Gabriel, but she never answered her phone. She left message after message, but she never gotten a return phone call back from Gabriel. She just prayed that Angel didn't have her goon squad to kill Gabriel. What Abby didn't know was it wasn't Angel who had Gabriel held hostage but it was Mr. Boris, another mafia kingpin that was about to let Gabriel and her mother go home because the job was completed, plus his revenge was sweet because Mr. Dane is dead. Now his family gets to feel the pain that he and his wife feel.

Mr. Boris was a man of his word; he had his bodyguards drop Gabriel and her mother off at a bus station and told them that they didn't owe any debt to the Russian family anymore. Once they made it home, Gabriel noticed her cell phone had at least fifteen missed calls, so Gabriel looked at her numbers and discovered that Abby had called ten times. Gabriel decided to call Abby after she takes a long, hot shower. While she was in the shower, images of Mike rubbing her pregnant stomach appeared in her head. She started to cry because not only did she lose Mike but now her father was dead too by the hands of her archenemy, Angel.

Abby wanted to call Gabriel one more time before she gave up calling her all together. She wanted so desperately to see if Gabriel was alive, and if she was, did she know that Mike was now dead. When Abby picked the phone up to call Gabriel for the eleventh time, Gabriel picked up the phone and said, "Hi, Abby."

Abby was so happy she started screaming in Gabriel's ear and said, "Gabriel, I thought that Angel had killed you."

Gabriel said, "I and my mother have been kidnapped by Mr. Boris, the head of the Russian mafia."

Abby said, "Oh my god, Gabriel, what the hell is going on. Did Angel join forces with the Russian mafia? Are you guys all right? Did they hurt you or your mother because the Russian mafia is more dangerous than any other crime family?" Abby was shooting question after question to Gabriel.

Abby was talking so fast until Gabriel said, "Abby, calm down, we're fine."

Abby and Gabriel were talking on the phone when they heard someone on the television show of the *Most Wanted* episode say they hand finally captured Angel Salvador a.k.a. Angel Carter. Abby and Gabriel were in awe because they never knew Angel as Angel Carter. They were trying to put their heads together to find out where this Angel Carter came in at. They both wanted to go back to Chicago to Angel's trial to find out the details of why they called her Angel Carter.

Gabriel asked Abby did she want to go to Chicago to see what they had on Angel and to see if she got accused of Mike's murder too. They agreed to meet at the airport the next morning on the first flight out to Chicago. When Abby and Gabriel made it to the airport, they looked at each other's stomach and were amazed that they were the same months.

Abby asked Gabriel, "What are you having, a boy or a girl?"

Gabriel said, "I am having a girl."

Abby told Gabriel, "I am having a little girl too."

They didn't have to ask about the father of their children because they both knew Mike had fathered both of their daughters.

When the plane touched down in Chicago, Abby and Gabriel rented a hotel room near the airport so they would be close to the airport if they needed to leave in a hurry. They got settled into their room and made plans to go to dinner together. When they finished dinner, they caught a cab to the courthouse for Angel's arraignment; they want to see if she was going to make bond.

Angel got charged with racketeering, murder, drug selling, black market baby-selling, and money laundering. Her bond was set at a million dollars, and St. Louis was there to bond her out, but they weren't going to let her out that easy. She had to go home on house arrest. St. Louis hired Angel a kick-ass attorney by the name of Steven Blake. He was a black criminal attorney that the prosecuting attorney hated because he won every case he ever took on. Steven Blake was a high-profile attorney. He also was an expensive attorney; he charged three thousand dollars an hour, and Angel paid every dime to make sure she didn't go to jail.

Angel got released from jail that morning of her trail. She was happy to be free for a while to hold her Baby Girl. While she was at home holding her daughter, the prosecuting team was digging up more dirt on Angel to make sure she never saw daylight again. Angel was so uptight while she was in her court hearing. All the things that they were saying about her that she didn't even notice Gabriel and Abby was there in the courtroom looking at her with death in their eyes.

Abby noticed that this woman was sitting there holding this pretty little baby in her arms while court was going on and Angel kept looking back at her. Abby or Gabriel didn't know that Angel had just had a baby, so when the women went to the restroom with the baby, Abby and Gabriel went right behind her to see what they both thought was true.

Abby said to the woman, "Oh, what a pretty little baby! Can I hold him?"

The woman said, "She's not a boy. She's a girl, and her name is Gloria Carter."

Abby and Gabriel were gasping ring for air; they couldn't believe that Angel had a baby, and was Mike her baby's father too.

Gabriel came up with an idea to kidnap Angel's baby to let her feel how it felt to lose someone you love. She told Abby what she was thinking, and Abby wasn't down with kidnapping Angel's baby, because she knew even while Angel was on trial for all these other things, she would still kill you, and to kidnap her baby would be a murder sentence for real, so she wanted no parts of it. Gabriel thought that Abby was so scary Angel put them through hell, and she didn't want to get her back, but Gabriel wanted some payback. She wanted Angel's heart to feel empty like hers. Gabriel didn't know Angel for real. Angel's heart has been empty for a long time. That's why she been going through the motion of all the bad things she's been doing.

Angel got up the next morning after being released from jail and started making arrangements for her daughter just in case Mr. Blake couldn't get her off her charges. She wanted to make sure little Gloria would be fine. She loved her daughter, and she made a promise to her that she would never go through what she went through. She also had a talk with St. Louis about changing his career path for the sake of their daughter because if she went to jail at least their daughter would have one parent that she could count on.

St. Louis told Angel, "Stop talking like that because we have an attorney that eats sharks for lunch, so stop tripping. You're not going to serve another day in jail. Just wait and see."

What St. Louis was saying to Angel made her think that her man had something stirring. She knew he was a master at getting things done, especially when it came to her, but what she didn't know was St. Louis had a hit out on everyone that was a part of Angel's trial, including the judge. He was going to make it a point that no one went up against Angel Carter.

Angel was sitting in her bedroom watching the news and breast-feeding her baby when a news reporter showed photos of the judge at Angel's trial was hanging from a bridge in downtown Chicago buck naked with a sheet wrapped around his neck. All Angel could think about was that she knew her man would look out for her. St. Louis was going down the list; he was on his way over to the prosecuting attorney's house while the news was still broadcasting the judge's murder. St. Louis had already had everyone that had been investigating Angel grabbed up and held until he got done with the jurors. He had been to all of their homes and burned them alive while they were sleeping.

Abby and Gabriel knew it was time to bounce. They said to each other, "This is some for real gangster shit going on here. Angel hooked up with a guy just as deadly as she is. We of all people know that St. Louis is a man that would kill you in a blink of an eye. He's been to jail on several occasions and never spent a day, so, Abby, you know that brother know people either in high places or he's killing everybody that has anything to with his cases."

Angel was feeling bad deep down inside. She really missed her girlfriends, but she couldn't get past the betrayal. They committed against her by sleeping with her boyfriend Mike, who Angel found out later that he was her brother by her father Cane, the Hawaiian kingpin. Angel thought to herself, I should call Abby and Gabriel just to see if those two bitches will answer my call, but what Angel didn't know was they wanted to talk to her, especially Gabriel, because she wanted to get close enough to Angel again to cut her throat for killing her father and her baby's father even if Abby didn't have the guts to do it.

Abby thought it was time to leave the Windy City. She was feeling tired and swollen up with carrying her baby. She had gained so much weight that she felt like the Goodyear blimp, plus she wanted to come back to Chicago when Angel trail started for the second time. She wanted her baby to be born before she visited the shy town again. Abby's and Gabriel's due dates were three days apart, and they promised each other that they would let their daughters grow up together as sisters.

Gabriel wanted to know for sure if Mike fathered Angel's daughter because she really didn't want her daughter to grow up alone if she was Mike's child, and if Angel went to jail, she figured maybe she could get custody of her and raise her with her sisters. Abby and Gabriel talked about Angel's daughter and what the child would have to go through if Angel went to jail, but what they were seeing on the news was devastating, because everyone that was on the law side of the trial was dropping like flies; someone was killing them all.

Abby told Gabriel, "Do you know Angel is having all of those people killed. You and I both know that Angel's elevator does not go all the way to the top floor. We really need to stop Angel. She need to pay for everything she's done, but if she doesn't get jail time, she going to burn in hell for what she's done for sure."

Abby was talking to Gabriel on the phone on a Monday night when her water broke. She started having labor pains soon after. Gabriel said, "Stay on the phone. I'm going to call an ambulance to come and get you. Just don't push, all right."

While Gabriel was on the phone with the ambulance people, her water broke as well. They sent an ambulance to pick up Gabriel too. Abby and Gabriel had two beautiful baby girls. They even weighed the same thing: eight pounds seven ounces and nineteen inches long.

Abby named her baby Sophia, and Gabriel named her daughter Michelle. She thought that it was as close as she could get to Mike. Their daughters looked so much alike it was scary. If Mike was alive, he couldn't deny either one of their daughters because they looked just like their father, the deceased Mike Trivet.

Chapter Sixteen
Isabella Stallone

ANGEL HAD GOTTEN so caught up in her trail that she had forgotten she had made appointment to meet with Helen Davis at the division of family services. She had told Helen that she wanted to donate some money to the families that was in need of help in the community housing. That's the only way she was able to get appointment so early with Ms. Helen Davis. When Angel arrived at the division of family services, they rushed her back to Helen's office. When Angel entered the office, Helen looked like she saw a ghost because her daughter Isabella and Angel could pass for twins.

Angel sat there looking at Helen before she said a word because she didn't want to just come out asking her questions about her father, so Helen asked Angel who was her parents because she looked so familiar to her. Angel told Helen her story of being a kingpin's daughter. She even told Helen about her mother. Helen couldn't believe what she was hearing.

Helen knew Cane was married when she started dating him. They were only seeing each other for a short while. He told her that he loved his wife, and he wasn't going to leave her. He just wanted to dibble around in the street for a while, but Helen fell head over heels in love with Cane, and she told him how she felt, and he told Helen that their little playtime was over. She was devastated; she was so upset about the turn of events with Cane. She became very sick. She had to be admitted in the hospital for observation and found out that she was pregnant.

Helen never wanted Cane to find out she was pregnant; she wanted him to stay away from her. It wasn't his fault that Helen caught feelings for him. He told her before they jumped in bed together that he had a family and he just wanted someone different than his wife to satisfy his sexual appetite. Hearing

Helen say all those things about her father made her want to throw up, but she kept her food down.

Angel finally decided to tell Helen who her father was. She was so calm because later she was going to make Helen hate. She even disrespected her mother, by sleeping with her husband, but right now Angel wanted to meet her sister. She wanted to get in contact with her. She saw a picture of Isabella sitting on her mother's desk, and she caught a headache instantly because that's the same Isabella that was dating her brother Dante. Angel said to herself, *Chicago is too fucking small. All the time she was right in my grill and I didn't even notice her.*

Helen told Angel that her daughter Isabella was a prosecuting attorney and worked downtown at Seventh District. Angel felt like she had been kicked in the stomach. *How could both daughters be on opposite sides of the law?* Angel called St. Louis to give him the information she just found out about her sister. She said, "Do you remember when I told you that my father had another daughter by this woman name Helen Davis?"

He said, "Yes. So what's up, Angel? Tell me, what's going on? Are you all right?"

Angel was on her way home when she called St. Louis. She kept looking out of her rearview window because she felt like she was being followed by a black Crown Victoria.

Angel told St. Louis what was going on, and he told Angel not to stop, keeping going until she make it home. He also told her that police detectives drive Crown Victorias.

He told Angel, "Don't worry about it. You make it home to me, and I'm gonna handle it once you get here. Hurry up, baby, I'm going to have the garage door up waiting on you to pull in."

Once Angel pulled into the garage, the Crown Victoria pulled up and sat across the street.

St. Louis went out of his back door with his Eagle machine gun and snuck up behind them and shot both men in the back of the head. He jumped in the car with the dead detectives and drove off. He drove about six miles down a dirt road and rolled their car off a deep cliff when the car hit the bottom of the cliff and exploded with fire and smoke. He said to himself, *Don't no one mess with my woman. Without consequences play with me and you will die.*

Angel was so worried when St. Louis didn't answer his phone, but she knew her man was smooth in whatever he did; his name should have been smooth. Angel had her sister Isabella's phone number. She wanted to call her for a lunch date at her house, but she didn't want to scare her off, because with all the press and camera crews hanging out around Angel's house these days, she knew Isabella knew what kind of person Angel Carter was, and by Isabella being on the opposite side of the law, she would have to be blindfolded to even enter Angel's house, period.

Helen had given her daughter a call as soon as Angel left her office because she didn't want her just walking up on her daughter. She knew Angel was bad news and a stone killer. She didn't really want her daughter to associate with the likes of Angel, but she did want them to meet each other at least once. Helen thought that Angel would be behind bars once her trial started anyway, so she didn't have to worry about Angel destroying her daughter's reputation.

Isabella knew more about Angel; she knew that Angel was a kingpin's daughter and she had killer instincts like a man on death row. She also knew that Angel was connected with St. Louis, the Chicago area drug lord. So she was bad news all the way around. Isabella's mother had told her that her father was a man named Harold Stallone who worked as a mechanic down on Broadway Street.

Helen thought about what her mother used to always say to her as girl: *What you do in the dark will soon come to light;* Helen couldn't do nothing but sit there and cry because what her mother said was so true: her dirt of sleeping with an Hawaiian kingpin had come back to bite her in the ass.

Helen made Angel promise her that she wouldn't tell her daughter about their father until she had a chance to tell her herself. She didn't want to admit that she should have told Isabella years ago, but Harold wanted to remain Isabella's father because when he met Helen, Isabella was only two weeks old. When Helen told Cane she was pregnant, he turned over his parental rights to Harold, so Cane never spoke of Isabella nor did he acknowledge she was his daughter.

Angel kept her promise; she met with Isabella, but she met with her on her turns. She wanted Angel to meet her at an art museum where there would be a lot of people hanging out. Isabella was stumbled that Angel wanted to meet her of all people. She wondered what she wanted to talk to her about because she wasn't the prosecutor on her case. So what on God's green earth did she have to talk with her about?

Isabella called her mother to let her know she was on her way to the art museum to meet with Angel Carter. She told Isabella to be careful and to watch her back because Angel had everyone in the tri-state area looking for her.

Isabella said, "I know, Mother. I'm not going to waste my time talking to a well-known killer like Angel Carter. She is wanted for all kinds of things. What's so messed is, her case came across my desk today—"

Before Isabella could say another word, her mother told her, "Let someone else try that case because someone is killing anyone that has enough nerves to stand up against Angel. So please, Isabella, let them white folks fight their own battles this time. Don't let them get you killed going up against Angel Carter. She plays for keeps. She has more soldiers than men on the whole police force.

Isabella thought long and hard about what her mother just said. She knew her mother was right; everyone on the police force was afraid to go after Angel Carter. They knew Angel had the power to even make the mayor of Chicago bow down to her, and if he didn't, she would wipe out his whole family. For some reason, Isabella felt that it was something important that Angel wanted with her, but she started to think maybe she knew her case came on her desk today. Isabella also knew Angel had all kinds of officials on her payroll, so she knew to keep whatever she knew about Angel's case to herself if she wanted to stay alive.

Angel played it off when she met up with Isabella about her relationship with Dante. She knew Isabella from dating her brother they didn't get a real chance to get anything started because Angel killed Dante three days after he and Isabella hooked up. Angel said, "I just wanted to meet with you because I haven't seen you since my brother's death. I always told Dante you were good people, and I know he liked you a lot because he told me so."

Isabella knew Angel was up to something. She could feel she wanted to tell her something, but she didn't spit it out but it was all good, because Isabella didn't want to be in Angel's company too much longer. She kept thinking about what her mother said: *Be careful and watch your back.* It kept playing over and over in her head like a recorder.

Isabella decided to cut the meeting short because her woman intuition kicked in and told her, *It's people out here who want Angel dead, and if you lay down with dogs, you get up with fleas.* That's something Isabella's grandmother used to tell her all the time, and why she heard her grandmother say it to her while she was sitting there talking with Angel made her tell Angel that she would have to call her office to set up a meeting the next time she wants to talk with her.

Angel looked at Isabella and said, "Bitch, do you know who I am?"

Isabella said, "Of course I do, bitch. You are a criminal who's wanted across the fucking map. So like I said, if you want to meet with me again, call my office for an appointment."

Angel was pissed; she never was the one to back down from a fight, but something about Isabella made Angel back the hell up. Angel liked the fact that Isabella wasn't scared of her in no shape, form, or fashion; she had heart, and Angel knew right then and there that she and her sister Isabella were Cane's daughter's, and if she could get Isabella on her side of the fence, they could really do some damage. Isabella knew Angel was after something, and she was going to find out what it was very soon.

Chapter Seventeen
Flipping the Scrip

ANGEL'S COURT DAY was coming up fast; she had two months to go before her trial started; she wasn't tripping off her trial at all because she was sure her man had taken care of everything. What she didn't know was since everybody on her case had been killed, she thought that it will be a while before they found someone to prosecute her case. Angel got a handwritten letter delivered to her house two weeks before her trial from the prosecutor's office saying she had been assigned a new prosecutor and her name was Isabella Stallone. Angel smiled to herself because she thought that she was holding the cards in her hand to shut Isabella down, and all she had to do is tell her attorney that Isabella and she were sisters and it was a conflict of interest and Isabella would be thrown off her case.

What Angel didn't know was her case was going to be the headline news for years to come because the one she trusted the most was the one to send her up the river for life. Isabella and St. Louis had been seeing each other for years. St. Louis loved Isabella; they planned this whole scenario with Angel. St. Louis was to become Angel's man and to gain her trust, but when she tried to rob his fortress, it took everything in him not to kill her. Isabella always knew who her father was; she even knew that Dante, David, and Angel were her family; she wasn't going to let her mother know because she was going to let her know the day before Angel's trial.

St. Louis met Isabella one day on his way to court; they been together for five years; they both played the newcomers that thought they were going to come to Chicago and take over. Isabella was to take Angel's case and make sure she didn't see daylight again; she even hooked up with Angel's attorney Steven Blake. He was getting paid by St. Louis to lose his first case. Steven Blake has money, but for St. Louis to come to him with a two-million-dollar deal on the table, he knew Angel was going up the river without a paddle.

Angel was waiting on all this madness to be over so she was more than ready when her court date came in. Two days away, she told St. Louis once the case was over they could get married and raise their daughter. What Angel didn't know was St. Louis and Isabella had enough information on her to send her to the gas chamber. St. Louis even took pictures of Angel killing the head of mafia family Mr. Salvador; she wiped out the whole family, including the dogs. He had recorded the whole street war killings of the Russian mafia they killed, but St. Louis was smart; he wasn't in any of the pictures. He had handed everything he had against Angel to Isabella. He wanted Angel gone. He didn't want her dead, but if they decided to give her the chair, it would be beyond his control.

St. Louis found out that Angel and Isabella were his sisters; he felt real green inside that he had a child with his sister, but he had news for both of them. He knew he had to keep Isabella around so he could stay out of jail, but when he found out that Isabella was trying to play him, he didn't have any more love for her. He did a background check on Isabella too and found out that she was put in the prosecutor's office by the Russian mafia she was setting him up to be killed as soon as they sent Angel to jail. So St. Louis had his brother, who we know as Steven Blake, to kill Isabella after Angel's trial.

Angel's trial started today, and everyone was there for the show, including Amy, Gabriel, and Abby. They all were there sitting in the first row waiting to see Angel get fried. The first testimony of the day was when the prosecutor called Aaron Morgan a.k.a. Hammer to testify against Angel. He was to tell the court what he did for the Salvadors. Hammer told the court he was Dante and David's right-hand man.

The prosecutor asked Hammer, "What do you mean right-hand man?"

Hammer told Isabella, "Well, in other words, I'm a hired killer."

"Mr. Morgan, can you tell the court what you did for the Salvadors on a daily basis and how much were you getting paid to be a hired assassin?"

"The Salvador family paid me three thousand dollars a week and two more thousand to be their chauffeur."

"So, Mr. Morgan, are you trying to tell the court that the Salvadors paid you five thousand dollars a week?"

"Yes, and I was paid by Angel Salvador to get rid of three bodies on June 3, which was the Russian guys she killed in the street war."

Isabella said, "All right, Your Honor, I rest my case."

The judge said, "Mr. Blake, would you like to cross-examine Mr. Morgan?"

Mr. Blake said, "No, You're Honor, not at this time, but I would like to call Amy Anderson to the stand, Your Honor."

Amy was shocked to see that they even knew she was there at first until she saw the mayor that she went to talk to about Angel, and even Mr. Hayes was there. He had information to put Angel away too. St. Louis had paid everybody off to get Angel out of the way.

When both of the attorneys did their closing argument, that's when the jurors went back in the back to come back with the verdict; everyone in the courtroom was on edge because if Angel was found guilty, she would be in jail for the rest of her life. St. Louis was sitting behind Angel at the defense table telling her it would be fine, knowing all the time he gave the prosecutor the nail to put in Angel's coffin.

When the jurors came back into the courtroom, the whole room got real quite waiting for the foreman to read the verdict. For the first time in Angel's life, she was afraid because they had her dead to right on everything she did, and the evidence they had was supposed to be tossed away by St. Louis. He was the only one that Angel would let get that close to her to even have that kind of information to bury her.

When the foreman stood up to read the verdict, Angel stood up with her attorney to hear her fate. When the foreman called off all guilty charges, the whole courtroom went crazy, especially Amy, Gabriel, and Abby. They knew she deserved everything that she got and then some. Angel was so devastated; she looked behind her for St. Louis; he was grinning in her face; he told Angel, "I was the one who gave them everything they needed to bury your ass with. Our father Cane was a shiest low-down dirty motherfucker, and you know what else, your attorney, Steven Hayes, say hi to your big brother. He's also a Carter."

Angel couldn't say anything after that. She just went numb because her whole life had spiraled out of control. Steven followed Angel in the back where she had to be booted and suited to be transferred to the women's prison. She was so shocked because she has to serve life with no possibility of parole, but she thought to herself, *That punk played me the whole time. We even had a baby together, but that's fine because payback is a bitch.*

Isabella though that by Angel being out of the way, she could slide in her place with St. Louis just until she got the code to his secret passage. Since Angel tried to rob him, he changed the whole room around. St. Louis had a dummy safe set up in place of the old one; he put two rockwilders in the place of the alarm systems so anyone that got in there would be in for a rude awakening.

Isabella was on her way out the courthouse when she ran into Steven Blake. He asked her if she wanted to have a celebration drink with him being as though she won the case. She was so excited that she won the case of the year. She said, "Why not? Let's go to Club Sexy. Do you want to drive or do you want me to meet you there?"

Steven said, "Since I asked you, I will appreciate if you ride with me and I will drop you back off at your car."

Isabella said, "Sounds like a plan. Let's go."

When they made it to Club Sexy, Steven told Isabella that he had to use the restroom. He snuck out the back door of Club Sexy, got in his car, and drove ten blocks to cut the brake line to Isabella's car. When he made it back to Club Sexy, Isabella was standing at a table talking to one of her associates about the case of Angel Carter.

Isabella saw Steven when he came out the restroom and she made her way back over to their table. What she didn't see was Steven putting a Mickey in her drink. She had ordered Steven a Hennessey and Coke, and she ordered herself an apple martini. They had two more drinks apiece before they were ready to go. Isabella started to feel a little light-headed, so Steven asked her would she be all right. Isabella assured Steven that she would make it home safely and that she would give him a call once she made it home to let him know she was at home. Steven walked Isabella to her car and watched her pull off. She was so dizzy from the Mickey, which Steven had put in her drink, until her vision was seeing only one side of the road.

Steven didn't hear from Isabella that night, but when he got up the next morning to shower for work, he turned on his television to hear the news: a report was just coming in about a woman hitting the side of the bridge and her car exploding killing the woman instantly. But the news reporter didn't mention the woman's name, so he didn't know for sure if it was Isabella yet.

Steven made it to office that morning on time. When he walked in, everyone was standing around looking like their best friend had died.

One of the attorneys asked Steven, "Did you see the news this morning?"

He said, "No, why?"

He said, "The woman that hit the bridge last night and her car exploded is Isabella Stallone."

Steven said, "You're kidding, right? Isabella and I had drinks last night, and I dropped her back off here to her car and she seem to be all right."

Isabella's mother Helen was distraught because she knew her daughter would be next. She warned her on several occasions to not take that Angel Carter case. Helen was so angry she wanted to go visit Angel in jail and kill her with her bare hands, but what she didn't know was Angel didn't have anything to do with the death of Isabella even though she wanted to. Steven went to visit his brother St. Louis to pick up his money for killing Isabella, but when he got to St. Louis's house, somebody had been there already and tore his house to shreds.

Steven had stepped back out the door as fast he could because he didn't know who tore up his brother's house, and he didn't want to get caught in a trap. He made it back to his car and took out his cell phone to call his brother. He answered on the second ring, he thought. The voice on the other end of the phone was a voice he never heard before. It sounded like a Russian speaking to him in a language he never heard before. The guy told him, "We have your brother, and he's going to die. Don't even offer a ransom because his life isn't worth it.

Steven was so distraught that he knew he was dealing with some heavy hitters, and he wanted nothing to do with it. A month had past, and Angel had heard why she was in jail now that Isabella was dead, and she wanted to see Steven so she could ask him to go check on her daughter, and she wanted him to know he set her up and hung her out to dry. She told Steven that she had billions of dollars in an overseas account, and if he helped her buy out her time, she wouldn't kill him.

Steven looked at Angel like she knew something that he didn't. Angel told Steven, "I know you been to your brother's house already and he wasn't there, huh? Well, he won't ever cross a rich bitch like me again, and I tell you something else, brother dear. If you don't have my conviction turned over tonight, when you close your eyes it will be your last."

Angel wasn't worried anymore about her daughter because the nanny she hired to take care of her daughter was set for life to take care of her if Angel got sent to jail. That's one of the arrangements that Angel took care of the day she went to court. Her daughter and her nanny were already on their way to Ohio, where her nanny was born. Angel had her daughter's nanny checked out thoroughly. She wasn't going to turn her child over to a psycho; she had to pretend that she was worried about her daughter to throw Steven off guard. St. Louis a.k.a. Ronald Louis was found dead with half of his head blown off sitting in a booth at Club Sexy on a Sunday night. He was put there by the Russian when the club closed that Saturday night. They never found his killer, and the police department didn't even try to solve his case. They looked at it like it has been another drug dealer bites the dust.

Chapter Eighteen
In Bed with the Enemy

STEVEN WENT TO visit Angel again in jail. This time he had a different agenda; he did his own investigation to find out about his biological father. He was told by his mother that Cane Carter was his father but, truth be told, his mother was alcoholic, and she had been to so many institutions for her drinking problems she didn't even remember having a child, so he was shipped off to his grandmother. Steven's grandmother raised him from the age of two until he graduated from high school. When Steven came home one day from signing up to go to college, he found his grandmother in the middle of the living room floor dead; she had a heart attack.

Steven buried his grandmother and went on to law school to become a kick-ass attorney. He graduated from law school with honors, and he opened up his own law firm and was well known to the people in the Chicago area. Steven did the investigation on the whereabouts of his real father, and, truth be told, his father was the commissioner of the Chicago police department. He had been working in the same circle with his father for years. It was a relief for Steven because he didn't want to be a kingpin's son; he really didn't want to be a commissioners son either, because how could a man of the commissioner's caliber have sex with a alcoholic woman he arrested for prostitution in the back of his squad car and drop her off in an alley and left her there like she was trash. Steven wanted to have a for real sit down with his father to pick his brain a little bit to see what kind of man he was. He didn't want to let him know he was his father just yet. He wanted to drop the bomb on him as soon as his proof was delivered to his office. He had a hair sample tested that he got from the commissioner's comb two days ago while the commissioner was out of his office for lunch. He snuck into the commissioner's office and stole his comb; he wanted to know for sure that the commissioner was his father before he blew the whistle on him as being his deadbeat dad.

Steven didn't really want the commissioner to own up to his responsibility of begin his father. He wanted him to own up to what he did to Steven's mother. When the test results came back to Steven's office, he was just a tad bit nervous because if he really was the commissioner's son, he was going to own up to want he did to Steven's mother, because, in Steven's eyes, his mother was raped by someone who is supposed to serve and protect the law, not abuse it.

Steven opened up the envelope, and to his surprise, it read Robert Harris's blood match is 99.99 percent match of Steven Blake, so it turns out that Steven's mother was right about telling her mother about what the commissioner did to her in his squad car that night. She also told her mother that she had been having sexual relationships with Cane the Hawaiian kingpin before he was killed too.

Steven had the evidence he needed to confront the commissioner, but he said to himself, *In time, I might need this information to buy me some time.* Steven thought about what Angel said to him, so he made another trip to the jail to visit her again. Deep down inside, he really cared about Angel; he liked her since the first day he took her on as his client, but he never was the type of guy to mix business with pleasure. When he went to visit Angel this time, he poured out his heart to her. Steven told Angel how he really felt about her. He even told Angel he wasn't her brother and he had proof.

She looked at Steven and said, "Why would I trust you? It was you and that barracuda sister of mine who put me in this place for the rest of my life."

Steven told Angel, "I'm going to get your case overturned, and if I do that, would you at least think about going out to dinner with me?"

Angel said, "If you get my case overturned, I would go to dinner with you, but I can't promise you that I'm going to forget that you helped put me behind bars."

Steven told Angel, "I'm going now to get started on your release. I have to go turn over some stones and grease some palms for this case to be over." He added, "I would be back to visit you in a couple of days."

He was on a mission, and it wasn't for God, but he sure was going to need God's help for sure.

Steven went to the commissioner's office first and laid down the law. He represented Angel like he should have done the first time. He told the commissioner that he had proof that could send the whole police department, some judges, mayors, and councilmen, and "you commissioner yourself has a dirty trail behind you too, sir."

The commissioner looked at Steven like "you may have a law degree and street-smart, but you don't have any right to come in my office and threaten me."

Steven got tired of arguing with the commissioner, so, instead, he said, "Look, I don't really have no conflict with you as of yet, so here's some information that I think you should take a look at. I want you to know I have tapes and video recorders that I have addressed to the Supreme Courts waiting to get mailed if something were to happen to me. There would be a paper trail leading to everyone that's involved in this madness. Since we're here talking, I need to ask you a question: 'Do you remember picking up a woman in your squad car for prostitution when you were a rookie cop about thirty-six years ago?'"

"Let me straight something out for you, young man. I can't remember what I ate for dinner yesterday, let alone remember some woman I met thirty-six years ago."

Steven was sitting in the commissioner's office. Getting heated, he said, "Mr. Robert Harris, I know for a known fact that you pick up this woman back in the day when you were a rookie cop. Her name was Tammy Blake. She's my mother you raped her, and I can prove it because I'm the result of that rape case."

Mr. Harris looked at Steven like he had just sprouted two heads. He asked Steven, "Are you crazy?"

Steven said, "I'm going to show you how crazy I am. If you don't help me overturn the case of Angel Carter, you're going to regret ever knowing Steven Blake."

Mr. Harris looked at Steven and said, "I don't know if I can help you. Her case was a high-profile case, and if we drag the case up again, it's going to be all kind of trouble for everyone that was involved."

Steven told Harris, "If you don't help me, everyone that was involved is going to be blown out of the water, including you. Does your wife know that just because you were a shield you think you have the power to go around raping helpless women and that you have a bastard son that is a a result to a rape case you committed?"

When Steven left the commissioner's office that day, the commissioner got on the phone calling in some favors to get Angel's case overturned. He knew by looking at his son that he meant business. He also got a good look at Steven. He knew before Steven gave him the results of the paternity test that he was indeed his father.

Mr. Harris had to get to the judges that were involved in the video movies that Steven had left him a copy of. Mr. Harris called the judges to set up a meeting with the judges in their chambers. When he made to the judge's chambers, both judges said, "This better be important, Harris, because we have work to do and trial's to hear."

Harris asked Judge Baker, "Can you put this tape in my hand in your recorder?"

Judge Baker said, "Go ahead, but this better be good, Harris."

When Judge Baker saw what showed up on the screen, he turned white as a sheet because he had no idea that Salvador's brothers were taping his sexual escapades. He was outdone; he couldn't do anything but shake his head in defeat. He knew he had to do something quick because his wife would divorce him, plus the media will eat him for lunch.

The commissioner said, "That's not all. We have you too, Judge O'Malley, staring in this video. Here, you are right here."

Judge O'Malley was the one getting screwed by a dog. It was disgusting to look at, but they had to watch it to see who had their balls clamp in a pair of vice grips. They all looked at each other in a state of shock.

Judge Baker broke the silence and said, "Harris, who did you get that tape from, and what do they want in return?"

"Well, Your Honor, I got the tapes from Steven Blake, and he said he has plenty more that he has ready to be mailed out to the Supreme Courts if we don't help him get Angel Carter's case overturned."

Judge Baker said, "Is Steven Blake crazy? Don't you know that we will get disbarred if that case even get looked at?"

"When Mr. Blake came into my office with this information, I didn't think that he had anything at first that was worth even looking at until he showed me the tapes. He has everyone by the balls, so either we play ball with him or we will be looking at jail time ourselves or worst."

Judge O'Malley said, "All right, we will meet up tonight at my house and come up with some light at the end of this tunnel because we all are facing some serious problems here."

All three men agreed to meet that night. Judge baker was so upset when the commissioner left his chambers. He wanted to go after Steven, but he knew better because he had too much to lose, plus he really didn't know for sure if Steven had letters ready to go out to be mailed to the Supreme Courts. Steven was in court on another case when he got a call from Judge Baker requesting that he meet him in his chambers as soon as possible. Steven thought to himself, *This better not be a trap, but just in case it is, let me call my people to let them know what's about to go down.*

Judge Baker told Steven, "You have guts to be messing around with the bigwigs." He added, "I hope you know what you're doing, son, because you are messing with fire."

Steven agreed with the judge he didn't deny what he was doing wasn't dangerous, but he just prayed everything would work itself out. Judge Baker let Steven know that Rome wasn't built in a day and trying to get a high-profile case overturned was going to take some time.

Steven Blake asked Judge Baker, "How much time you are talking about because time is of essence. My client has a life she wants to get back to."

"Mr. Blake, 'when' and 'if' your client get released, how would we know that those tapes won't get sent to the Supreme Courts anyway?"

"First, let me correct you, Your Honor. It's 'when' my client get released."

"All right, Mr. Blake. When your client gets released, what's going to happen to those tapes is what I'm worried about."

"You have my word. That those tapes won't get released to anyone unless you guys get it in your minds to come after me or my client."

Judge Baker thought about what Steven said and said, "I guess, we should get the ball to rolling on your client's release, but we have one stipulation, that is for your client to leave the city of Chicago. She's not welcome here anymore, so upon her release, she has to cash out on everything she owns and get out and never return again."

Steven went to visit Angel to let her know that she would be getting out soon and to let her know to be patient. Angel was so happy to see that Steven could make it happen so fast, but what she hadn't figured out yet that it was going to be a year later before the judges could get all the paperwork situated. Steven never thought in a million years that he would be in bed with the enemy, but he made a promise to himself that he hoped he never have to cross paths with the bigwigs again. Steven knew once Angel got released, he would have to take his law firm somewhere else to start over because with that many people coming after him he wasn't going to have a healthy growing business.

The city of Chicago was never going to be the same it was to many illegal officials running that town to the ground, and the people who made the town didn't have a voice. Everyone was afraid to speak out loud to anyone that they thought could stop what was going on, but it was no one they could trust; the whole town was corrupted.

Chapter Nineteen
Angel s Release

ONE YEAR LATER, Angel Carter finally hitting the streets. When she heard her name being called to pack it and stack it, she really didn't know what that meant until one of the guards hollered out and said, "Angel Carter, let's roll you being released." She was ecstatic she couldn't believe that Steven Blake had kept his promise, and she was going to keep hers by having dinner with him. She was as hungry as a hostage. When she made it to the front desk to get her things, Steven was there waiting on her. She looked at him and smiled. He thought she had the most beautiful smile he has ever seen. Angel had other plans for Steven. She wanted her back cracked, and he was the best man for the job.

Angel made plans to be out of Chicago in two weeks, but first, she had to get her affairs in order. She contacted a friend of hers she met two years ago. He was someone she kept on standby for emergency. He too was a heavy hitter and was an assassin for the Columbian mafia. He always cared deeply for Angel, but he never forced the issue. He knew one day she would need him and whatever the situation was he would be there for her, and Angel knew he would be. Angel called Ramon to see if she could talk to him about her situation on selling her assets. Ramon told Angel to come and see him; he already had her covered.

Angel was about to go to the airport to catch a flight out to Columbia. When she got to the airport, Ramon was standing there looking sexy as hell. Angel said, "Damn, Ramon, you still fine as homemade wine. I thought that you wanted me to come to you. I just did that to see if you would come to Columbia. Now that I'm here, let's go have lunch and wrap up your situation with selling your assets."

Ramon told Angel, "It's a way around selling your assets what do you really want to do because I kept up with the news while you were on lockdown, and the state of Chicago want you to get the hell out of dodge."

Angel told Ramon, "Yes, they do, and it's cool because my plan was to leave for a while anyway to strategize my next move. You know me, it's not over to Angel Carter, say it's over I have some unfinished business here in Chicago, and they're not going to get rid of me that easy."

Ramon had already looked into some dummy corporations for Angel because she didn't want to get rid of none of her properties. She had those six apartment buildings, two stores, and a club. She wanted to make the judges think she sold everything and left town.

Angel knew one thing for sure that they would check to see if she got rid of her assets, so she went on and set up the dummy corporations up under a fictitious name, and her assets would be filed under a assumed name she had a company set up as Top of the Line Inc. Ramon went along with Angel's title for her company because he thought it suited her because she carried herself just like she named her company Top of the Line.

Angel and Ramon stayed in touch with each other daily. She packed up all her things and left the Windy City. Her first stop was to go to Ohio to get her daughter, and she was moving to California for a while. When she got to Ohio, her daughter and her nanny was out at the park. When the nanny pulled up into her driveway, she didn't see Angel sitting outside her house. She was too busy hitting at Angel's daughter sitting in the backseat of the car. When Angel saw the nanny hit her daughter, she went ballistic. She hadn't seen her daughter in a year, and to see her nanny hitting her child, she wanted blood. Angel couldn't wait until she got in the house. She went up to her car and put her forty-four up to her head and told her, "Bitch, leave my daughter in the car. You and I are going to step into your house." The nanny was scared because she didn't even know that Angel had got released. She had been beating on Angel's daughter for a while, but now that Angel was back, it was time to find out what she had been doing to Angel's daughter.

Angel was pissed, and the nanny knew it. When Angel got the nanny in the house out of her daughter's view, she asked her nanny, "How long you have been putting your hands on my daughter? And before you answer think about it, because if you lie to me, I'm going to put your brains all over your stainless steel refrigerator."

The nanny actually thought that if she tells the truth, Angel wouldn't kill her, so she told Angel she would get beaten twice a day, because she would cry for nothing, and she wasn't going to put up with that kind of behavior before the nanny could finish her sentence. Angel slapped her so hard across the face with the back of her forty-four pistol. Angel said, "Bitch, you should have lied to me because you would never be a nanny to another agency again because your number has just been deleted."

Angel went back to the nanny's car, took the car seat out, put it in her car, and put her daughter in the car seat, buckled her up, and drove off. When Angel drove off, she didn't think about the nanny's neighbors hearing the gunshots at the time. She was pissed at what she witnessed the nanny doing to her daughter. The next-door neighbor did hear the shots and called the police right away. She also gave a description of the car Angel was driving, which was a dark blue Ford with Chicago plates.

Angel knew someone heard the gunshots. That's why she stole the car before she left Chicago. In her mind, she knew something was wrong because she had a gut feeling before she made it to Ohio to pick up her Baby Girl that she might have to do some harm to somebody, but she didn't think it was going to be her daughter's nanny. Angel ditched the car and stole another one, and when she made it out of Ohio, she stopped by a car lot and bought a Ford Explore and made it to San Diego, California, where she set up camp for a while.

Angel rented an apartment because she wasn't going to make California her home. She was just visiting. Angel thought to herself, *after I get settled, I would give Steven a call to see how he was doing.* But before she even had two days to get settle, Steven called Angel to let her know that he had just moved to San Diego to start up his new law firm. Angel didn't know rather to be happy or sad because even though Steven helped her get released, he also was the reason why she got sent away. Steven asked Angel where was she. And she really didn't want to tell him that she was staying in San Diego too, but she told him anyway it wasn't like he couldn't find out anyway.

Steven admired the fact that he and Angel were in the same state, so he thought he had a chance to become more than just Angel's friend. He had plans to get close to her daughter as well. He didn't have any children and becoming a father to Angel's daughter would be a start. Steven asked Angel if he could come by and see her and her daughter and bring dinner along with him.

Angel said, "Of course, you could come by. I need some company. Maybe I can relax a little with some adult conversation."

Steven told Angel that he would be there at seven. He also asked her would Chinese food be okay.

She said, "I'm sure it would be for us, but I don't think it would be proper food for my daughter. She's only one."

Steven said, "All right, how about I stop at the grocery store and pick up some baby food."

Angel said, "No. But thanks anyway she has plenty of baby food here already."

Steven said, "All right, is there anything else you want me to bring?"

Angel said, "Yes, you can bring a bottle of white wine with you."

Steven said, "Will do see you at seven."

Angel was sitting there watching the news when her doorbell rung. It was Steven; he was very prompt with being on time. While Angel was standing there directing Steven to the kitchen, she heard a news reporter say that they had found a woman in the Ohio area that had been shot in the face with a forty-four; her face was completely blown off. Angel stood there looking with this half-smile on her face saying to herself, *That bitch will never hit another child, especially not mine.*

Steven and Angel had a nice dinner together; they retreated from the kitchen into the living room where they finished off that bottle of wine. Angel started feeling hot and bothered she gave Steven the eye letting him know it was okay to make a move if he wanted to. Before she could get the thought out of her mind, Steven was all over Angel. She didn't even stop him to strap up. She thought to herself, *What the hell, I'm not going to get pregnant.*

Angel started seeing Steven on a regular basis. They did a lot of things together with her daughter. She started feeling like a family, but she couldn't shake the feeling that he hung her out to the wolves. Angel knew it can never be anything serious with her and Steven because she would never trust him, and one day, she was going to—have to, kill him. Steven and Angel were at the mall one evening when she saw Abby pushing a baby in a stroller. Angel really wanted to go over and speak to Abby. Angel said, *What the hell, she has her baby with her and I have mine, so it's not going to be any arguing around the children, plus I need her to see me and my spouse-to-be attorney Steven Blake.*

Abby was nervous as hell when Angel walked up on her. She knew that Angel was deadly; her killing her in the middle of the mall wouldn't stop Angel if she wanted her head. Abby thought that she would just play it cool just to see what Angel wanted to say to her. She was shocked because Angel spoke to her and asked, "What's your daughter's name?"

"My daughter's name is Sophia."

Abby knew not to take any chances with Angel because she is one deadly female and to be face-to-face with a known killer is dangerous.

Abby knew going up against Angel is like going up against guerrilla warfare. She knew that as big as California was she had to move away from there as soon as she got back home. When Abby got back to her apartment, she started packing as fast as she could. She jump in her car and headed back to Hawaii.

She called her mother and told her she had just seen Angel in the mall with her attorney slash boyfriend. Abby told her mother that she didn't even know Angel was out of jail. She also told her mother that it's something strange going on because what they had on Angel she should be behind bars for the rest of her life.

Angel was fueled with fire when she ran up on Abby at the mall; she wanted to drop Abby where she stood for real. Angel thought about the day she got sentence when she saw Abby and Gabriel sitting there smiling at her like they were glad she was going to prison for the rest of her life, but what they didn't know was she was going to get released.

Angel lay awake that night thinking of a master plan she still had some business to take care of in the Windy City, and she was going back there to take care of some loose ends, and she also had some people there that she wanted to rock to sleep, so Angel's mind was on overload. She had to come up with a new identity, so when she stepped back into Chicago, no one would have never heard of Angel Carter. While Angel's mind was wondering around all over the place, all of a sudden a light popped on in her head it was time to call a surgeon to construct her whole body with a makeover. She didn't want to waste not one more night of sleep trying to get back at the people who tried to seal her faith.

Angel sold off her assets to her dummy corporation and she was set on that end. All she had to do was get her body well from her makeover and she would be on her way back to the Windy City of Chicago. Angel even decided to change the color of her eyes to hazel brown to match her semi-light blonde hair. She wanted to look sophisticated and elegant; she wanted everyone that was involved in her case to be thrown off guard by her beauty. She got on the Internet that night because she had seen an ad about a two-bedroom loft on the outskirts of Chicago that she wanted to purchase for now. Angel wanted her come back to be bold and with a statement that she's Angel Carter and don't ever forget it.

Angel didn't trust anyone; she went on and bought the loft and had it locked down like New York state prison system. She was back and in charge. She had a theft-proof computer system. She even had a bank security system put in her bedroom closet where she kept some cash, but she kept a lot of her cash in offshore accounts. Angel was ready to start a fire in Chicago that they never saw before. She didn't want to hurt innocent people, but the ones she was after was going to burn in hell for every day she spent behind bars. Angel even bought her a white Cadillac truck. She even bought her a white Mercedes. She wanted to make them think she was an investor real estate broker buying and selling property.

Angel had cards made up with her picture on them. She would also go to

Club Sexy every weekend and talked the owner of Club Sexy to selling it to her dummy corporation for a hundred thousand dollars in cash. That was her first move. She wanted her mother's club back in the family. She met up with the owner of Club Sexy that morning at a hotel. He came with the deed to the club, and Angel showed him the hundred thousand dollars. When he reached down to grab the suitcase, Angel came up from behind him and cut his throat from ear to ear. He bled to death right there in the hotel room on the floor. Angel didn't feel no remorse because he took over her mother's club without any remorse so why should she have any for him, plus he stole her mother's deed to the club out of her safe. He even had the nerve to white out her name and put his on the deed as the new owner so he had that coming.

Angel was on alert like a shark in a shark tank on a eating frenzy. She was harboring so much hate inside her she wanted everyone to pay one by one; her next victim was her attorney, Mr. Hayes. He had given her sister the prosecuting attorney Isabella Stallone information on her too. She always thought that client–attorney privilege meant that everything between you and your attorney was private, but no, Mr. Hayes took her privacy to a whole another level and for that he was going to die in public for everyone to see.

Angel made appointment with Mr. Hayes as a new client; she pretended like she wanted him to find her lost brother. He looked at Angel like she was an angel that had fallen from grace; he couldn't stop his leg from shaking; he was a nervous wreck. Angel gave him some fake information that lead him to a vacant house where she would be there waiting on him. When he arrived at the vacant building, it didn't look empty, so Mr. Hayes went inside only to see Angel standing there dressed in all red. She said look at me real good because this is going to be the last time you see anything in life. Mr. Hayes was afraid because he remembered her voice now, but he didn't remember her voice when she was in his office earlier.

When Angel stepped out in the light so he could see her, he almost passed out because he too thought Angel Carter was doing time on Rikers Island. Angel said, "Don't look stupid now. When you were in court, you spoke loud and clear and with confidence that I was a stone killer, but you know what that part was very true because what I'm about to do to you now they will see you for the asshole you really are." Angel had her twin Rutgers machine guns strapped to her side. She told Mr. Hayes to take off his clothes and threw them over to her; he did what he was told because he saw Angel in action he knew not to play with her. He took off his clothes and threw them to Angel. Angel told him to get down on all fours. She had broken off a broomstick and stuck the handle up to Mr. Hayes's ass to show him how it felt to get fucked. After MR. Hayes was through screaming, Angel took off his penis with a switchblade. She then took his body and shoot holes all through his corpse. After Mr. Hayes went limp, she pulled his body to the street where she hung him from a tree right in front of the vacant building for everyone to see. She even left a note attached to his dead chest that read: "here goes the worst attorney to ever be hired as a lawyer."

Chapter Twenty
Angel and Steven Blake

ANGEL LEFT **C**HICAGO after three weeks and went back to California. She was happy to get a goodnight's sleep. Once she made it home, she was exhausted, took a shower, and went to bed. She woke up the next morning and made breakfast for her and her Baby Girl. As they were eating breakfast, her telephone started ringing. She looked at the caller ID and said it's Steven.

She answered, "Hi, Steven."

He said, "Good morning, Angel. What are your plans for today?"

Angel told Steven, "I had planned on taking my Baby Girl to the zoo and after that we are going to have lunch at McDonald's."

"Oh, that sounds like a plan. Well, I'm working today, and if you are free later, I would love to come and visit my best two girls today, if you don't mind."

"Well, I'll call you when we get back home. I have to go, Steven. I'll talk to you later."

When Angel hung up with Steven, she and her Baby Girl headed out the door and didn't really want Steven to come over. She wanted to put a little distance in between them. Angel was pushing her daughter through the zoo when she heard footsteps behind her, and when she turned around to see who it was, it was this tall, dark, and handsome guy dressed to impress. He smelled good enough to eat.

He looked at Angel and smiled and said, "Slow down, sexy lady, I've been following you since you entered the zoo. Hi, my name is Wallace."

"Oh, I'm sorry. My name is Angel, and this is my daughter, and her name is Gloria. She's a cutie."

"I was wondering if I could take you to beautiful ladies out to lunch."

"Well, you could take us, but I will be driving my own car, okay? I would just follow you."

Angel drove to McDonald's like she promised with her daughter. When she pulled up at McDonald's, Wallace didn't have second thoughts. He just looked at the situation like this was for the benefit of the baby.

When Angel had finally left McDonald's, she thanked Wallace for lunch and told him she would see him later.

He said, "Hold on a minute, baby. Can I get your seven digits before you go? Maybe we can do this again real soon."

Angel said, "Sure, we can hook up some time when you're not too busy with your woman."

"Oh, it's not like that I have a girl, but we're on the outs right now, but it's all good. My woman is not the problem, I am."

Angel smiled because she liked his swagger and boldness. He was her type of guy. He was rough around the edges, so she knew he was a keeper.

Angel made it home and gave her daughter a bath and put her down for a much needed nap. When Baby Girl went to sleep, Angel went into her living room, put on some Luther Vandross, and was singing to his songs when her doorbell rung. She said to herself, *I wonder who the hell this is ringing my doorbell like they crazy.* When Angel peeped through the peephole of her door, she was disgusted to see it was Steven. He came over to her house without calling first; she was pissed.

Angel asked Steven, "What are you doing here, Steven? Plus you just can't come to my home without calling."

"Angel, I didn't mean no disrespect. I just thought that I would come by and surprise you, that's all. I went and bought the baby a few things that I thought she would like."

"Steven, first of all, don't ever come to my house without calling again, and second, of all my daughter has more stuff than any child I know. Thanks for thinking about her anyway. I appreciate the thought."

Steven didn't like the fact that Angel snapped on him. The way that she did, he wanted to stress the fact it was him that made it happen for her to even have a home to come to. When Angel noticed the expression Steven had on his face, she knew he had some ill feelings he was holding inside, but he didn't say anything, so she didn't push the issue in what he was thinking. While Angel was sitting in the living room talking with Steven, her phone rang. She picked up the receiver and said hello when she heard the deep voice on the other end. She knew it was Wallace.

He said, "What's up, sexy lady? What's on the agenda for today?"

She said, "Whatever you want to do."

Wallace said, "Damn, I like your style. So let me get your address and I'll call you before I come your way. Right now I'm at my cousin's house recording my demo."

"Oh, so you can sing for sure?"

"Sweetie, I can blow."

"All right, Wallace, I will see you later on. Call me when you get ready to holler at me, okay?"

When Angel hung up the phone with Wallace, Steven looked like he had swallowed a canary. He was pissed at Angel, and he wanted to know who this guy was she had just hung up with.

He asked her, "Who is Wallace?"

She said, "First of all, I don't owe you an explanation of who I'm talking to. That's none of your business. You're not my man, you were my attorney, remember, and now you better be careful in what you say to me because you my brother are treading on thin ice."

Steven was so angry when he left Angel's house that he thought it was time to do some investigation on this Wallace character because he didn't want anyone coming between him and Angel. He said to himself, *I have invested a lot of time in you and have poured out my feelings to you about how I feel about you, so I am not about to let no want-to-be player or drug dealer come snatch my woman away from me.* Steven called Angel that night to see if she was at home, but when he didn't get an answer, he just drove over to her house and sat down the street to see who she was with. When she came home, Steven sat outside Angel's house for four hours before Angel and Wallace pulled up. When they pulled up, Wallace carried Angel's daughter in the house and lay her down on the couch. Angel followed close behind Wallace; he didn't stay in the house long; once he came out the house, Steven followed Wallace to his house. He wanted to find out who this hood nigger was trying to roll up on his woman. Steven didn't have no idea that Wallace was for real a thug; he was strictly a hustler, and he drops niggers for just looking at him funny.

Steven decided to call Angel to see if he could try to explain to her about his feelings for her one more time. When he called Angel, she told him to come on over because she had some things to discuss with him too. When he made it to Angel's house, she was standing at her front door waiting to let him in. He spoke as he entered the front door, and Angel just bowed her head; she wanted to set the record straight with Steven.

Angel asked Steven, "Do you want anything to drink before we start our conversation?"

He said, "Sure. Can I have a bottle of water? That would be fine."

Angel went in her kitchen and got two bottles of water, and they headed to the living room to sit down. Angel said Steven, "you and I are just friends. Yes, we slept together a couple of times, and we both had a sexual enjoyment out of it, but now that the thrill is gone, so am I, I've, moved on and you need to do the same. We can still remain friends if you want, but that thing with friends with benefits is history. I've dealt you my last card."

Steven was blown out the water with what Angel had just said to him. He was angry enough to spit in her face but to take that chance would be death a mental to his health, so he left Angel's house with hate in his heart and killing in his mind. Angel knew Steven was angry with her, but she could care less she knew one day it would come to that, and she was more than happy to put his ass to that test.

Steven thought, *If I couldn't have Angel, Wallace sure not going to have her either.* Steven even said, *If I kill her, I would just have to adopt her daughter as my own.* While Steven was thinking about killing Angel, she was thinking the same thing about him. She had made up her mind that day he left her house that it was well past time to send Steven Blake straight to sleep. He had worked her last nerve, and it was time for him to kiss the world good-bye.

Angel had a kidnapping scheme going on in mind for Steven. She wanted to call him to meet her for one more last roll in the hay. She knew he wouldn't pass up the opportunity of sleeping with her. She did just that. She called Steven, and he went running. He had an idea of his own he was going to choke Angel out while they were having sex, but he didn't know Angel had a plan of her own too. She had a hotel room already reserved for them at the Hilton. She also hired a female hooker who resembled her. While they were in the room, Angel went hiding in the closet. She already went to the room to set things up. She had candles lit up everywhere. The hotel room was dark; nothing wasn't flowing through there but candlelight's.

Angel made sure not to get seen by anyone sneaking into the hotel. She had her thirty-eight snug nose with a silencer on it. She even took her switchblade just in case. When Steven got to the hotel, Angel's look-alike had already made her entrance. She lay across the bed. When Steven knocked on the door, she said "come in, Steven, the door is open."

When Steven stepped in the room and saw this naked body lying across the bed, he said, "I hope you haven't started without me."

The look-alike said, "No, baby, I was just waiting on you, but now that you are here, I don't have to wait no longer. Come over here to me, baby, my body is heated. Let's get this party started."

Steven had bought a bottle of red wine with him. He said, "Can I open our bottle of wine first?"

She said, "Sure, the glasses are over on the table."

He popped the bottle, and poured them a glass of wine. Steven took off his clothes and slid between the sheets. He pulled Angel's look-alike on top of him and kissed her with his eyes closed. He never opened his eyes once to see who really was on top of him.

Steven broke the kiss and said, "Roll over, baby. I want to hit it from the back."

She rolled over, and Steven started talking saying, "You sure you want all this meat to go to waste knowing you can get it as long as you want it?"

When the look-alike was about to answer him, Angel busted out the bathroom. She told Steven, "Take your dick out slow and turn around. Move over to the chair."

When he did, Angel tied him up with his dick still hanging.

Angel moved over to the bed where her look-alike was setting, and she said to her, "Good job, but I can't leave any wittiness." And she stuck her thirty-eight in her mouth and blew her head off and blood went all over the hotel wall.

When Angel was done with her look-alike, she went back over to the chair where she had Steven tied up. She took off her pants. She told Steven, "I'm going to give you a ride of your life before I kill you, because in reality, you do have some good dick, but don't worry, I'm going to make it quick. I hope you can bust your last nut because I'm taking your family jewels with me to keep as a reminder of how good you were in bed. I want you know that when I meet up with Wallace tonight I'm gone to rock his world and you can take that to the bank."

When Angel was done riding Steven to an orgasm, she had already had her pistol up to his head the whole time. Once she had her orgasm, she pulled the trigger and shot Steven in the right temple of his head, and he just dropped his head to the side and took his last breath. He was gone just like that.

Chapter Twenty-One
Angel and the Columbian Mafia

RAMON WAS SITTING back talking with his uncles when Angel name came up. One of his uncles wanted to hire Angel as their own personal assassin; she was good at being a female killer. She slid through the night like the darkness. They wanted Ramon to invite her to Columbia for a visit, and they wanted to drop some knowledge on Angel. Also they really wanted Angel to be a part of their organization. Ramon didn't know for sure if Angel would take them up on their offer, but he knew he wanted Angel to be his wife, but he didn't want her the way that she was. She would have to do a whole lot of changing for her to be wife material. Ramon knew Angel like the back of his hand. He knew she was deadly. Without question, he also knew she wasn't the one to be played with. She killed her whole family that was mafia, and she even killed at least twenty Russians from the Russian mafia family. Right now Baby Girl is a hot commodity, and she has her plate full, but Ramon's thought was to take some of the load off her shoulders. That way she has some time for him.

He put the call in to Angel like his uncles requested, and to his surprise, Angel accepted because she wanted to see Ramon. She haven't seen him since he left Chicago, and her body yearned for his touch. Angel and Ramon never slept together, and she was going to make sure this wasn't going to be a wasted trip. She was finally going to see what Ramon had on his mind. Angel was on a date with Wallace when Ramon called her. She told Wallace she had to take the call and excused herself from the table.

She went outside to talk to Ramon when he asked her, "Are you ready to come to Columbia to visit me?"

She said, "Yes. When do you want me to come?"

He said, "What about tomorrow? I can pay for your ticket on this in or I could fly out on our private plane to get you."

Angel said, "Well, I tell you, what you can do is come pick me up in your private plane. That would be even better."

Ramon said, "It's not a problem. I will be there in the morning around ten, and I will have my driver bring me by your house to pick you and your daughter up, how's that?"

Angel said, "It's a plan. I'm going home right now to pack our things."

Ramon said, "Aren't you at home right now?"

Angel said, "No. I'm on a date with this guy I just met. He seems all right for now, but he's not my guy or anything. We are just kicking for now."

Ramon said, "All right, but cut your visit short with your friend and go home and pack."

"All right," Angel said, "yes," and they hung up.

The next day, Ramon was there on time like he said. He was standing at Angel's door at ten thirty. She opened her door and saw Ramon standing there. She started smiling like a little schoolgirl.

Ramon said, "What's up, ma? You ready to roll out?"

Angel said, "Of course, but I need to go into my room to get the suitcases."

Ramon said, "No. That's why I have my man Hotwire right here. Just show him where your room is and he will take them to the car."

Hotwire went and got the bags put them in the car, and they were on their way to Columbia.

Angel was happy to be in the company of Ramon, so whatever he said wouldn't matter because quiet as kept she had a mad crush on Ramon, but she thought that he wasn't interested in her. Ramon wasn't going to tell Angel that he past his crush stage, and with her his feeling toward her was emotional. Now since she was on his turf, he was going to show her what she meant to him and more he wanted to lavish Angel's body from head to toe. He wanted to drink her juices and swallow her whole, but that too would have to wait until his uncles had their time with Angel, but he couldn't keep his eyes off her. She was beautiful to him, and he knew his uncles would admire her as well.

When Angel walked into Ramon's uncle study, all three of his uncles kissed Angel's hand. They all greet her with a big smile. They thought she was gorgeous, and she would be the perfect assassin, but they first had to get her to cross over to their organization. They didn't talk business that night. They let her get comfortable before they dropped business on her, plus they could tell that their nephew had eyes for her, so they let him work his magic on her first.

Ramon was talking so sweet and sexy to Angel she didn't know if she is coming or going. The only thing she could say was damn, he was sexy. They went for a walk on the beach while the housekeeper took care of Angel's daughter. Ramon had the chef to make them a little snack with a bottle of white wine. Ramon had a blanket laid out on top of the sand ready for them to sit down on, but Angel had other things in mind. She wanted to wrap her legs around his waist and let it do what it does. Ramon wasn't going to let it go down that way. He wanted Angel in his bed, not on beach sand where everyone could see. She was more important to him than just a fuck.

Angel had drunk so much wine until she didn't even remember going back to Ramon's estate. She thought they were still on the beach. Ramon took Angel back to his estate. When she passed out from all the wine she consumed, he undressed her and put her to bed in his guest room. When he was ready to make love to Angel, she wasn't going to be intoxicated. He wanted her sober, so she would know when he entered her private garden.

When Angel woke up the next morning, her head was rocking. She had a headache that wouldn't quit, so she asked the maid for an aspirin, when the maid went to get Angel an aspirin. She heard her Baby Girl laughing. She wondered who had her laughing like that, and before she could force herself to stand up, Ramon came into the bedroom with the baby on his shoulder, and they both were grinning from ear to ear. She was happy to see someone like Ramon showing interest in her daughter.

Ramon invited Angel downstairs for breakfast. She told him she was going to take a quick shower and would be right down. He said all right and disappeared out the door with her daughter. When Angel made it downstairs to breakfast, she all most cried because the table was set up just the way the Salvador family used to have theirs. The memory she had of them made Angel sick to her stomach because it all was a big lie.

Ramon sat next to Angel, and he kissed her forehead. He said, "It's all right, ma. I got you from here on out nothing are no one is going to make you second-rate again." Angel smiled because if nothing else, she knew in her heart that Ramon felt something for her, but she wasn't sure if it was love yet, because she had been hurt before, and she wasn't going to move to quick on trusting her heart. She wanted it to just play itself out because time would tell for real.

After Ramon and Angel finished eating breakfast, they were to meet Ramon's uncles in the study to talk business. Angel was little worried because she didn't know what these Columbian mafia kingpins wanted from her. When Ramon's uncle Leo told Angel he wanted her to join their organization as their female assassin, she was stunned because she never thought of herself as assassin. She thought of herself as a killer, but to put a name to it was hilarious. Angel couldn't believe what they had just said, so she asked them "why me?"

Uncle Leo said, "Because no one would ever expect you because you come in the night like a ghost, and we never had a female in our organization that was heartless like yourself."

"If I were to take you guys up on your offer, what will be my job as your personal assassin?"

"You will be on call to hit wherever we want you to hit, so this means you would be on call twenty-four hours a day."

Angel asked Uncle Leo, "My price would be a half a million dollars a job, and if I have to go out of state, I need your plane to get me to my destination, and my daughter comes first, no ifs, ands, or buts about it. If my daughter gets sick or hurt and she needs me, I'm going to be there for my daughter. Everything else is secondary. Do we have a deal? Because if not I'm backing out of this organization right now."

Ramon's uncle looked at Angel, and he smiled and everyone else in the room followed suit. Angel was tough, but they agreed to her terms, and Angel was now a Columbian female assassin for the Columbian mafia.

Chapter Twenty-Two
Angel: The Columbian Female Assassin

ANGEL LEFT COLUMBIA after staying there for a week. She was now officially a female assassin hired by the Columbian mafia. Ramon flew her back home to California; she was getting ready for bed when her phone rung; it was Wallace. He had been calling Angel while she was in Columbia, and she wasn't answering her phone or returning none of his calls, so he was worried about her. So when she answered the phone, he was happy to hear her voice.

Angel told Wallace, "I am fine, and my phone don't have any reception where I am."

He said, "Okay, but if you don't mind, can I ask you were you disappeared to overnight?"

Angel had to clear a few things up with guys asking her questions about her own personal space.

She said, "Excuse me, I don't like twenty-one questions. I'm not your woman and you're not my man. If I don't ask you your whereabouts, please don't ask me mine. Now I know that's not the reason you woke me up out of a peaceful sleep to question me."

"Well, I just wanted to know if you were all right. Now that I know you good, I will call you tomorrow if that's all right with you, ma."

Angel said, "Goodnight, Wallace, I'll talk with you tomorrow, all right?"

He said okay, and Angel hung up, with Wallace still holding the phone to his ear.

Wallace didn't like Angel checking him like he was some little punk, so he said the next time he saw her, he was going to put her in her place. Little did Wallace know he wasn't going to check Angel. He was going to get dismissed if he thought he was going up against Angel. The next morning wasn't coming fast enough for Wallace. He woke up early because he couldn't rest last night thinking about how Angel shut him down. He never had a female to check him, and it wasn't going to start now; she had him all the way twisted.

Angel was on her way out the door when she heard car wheels screeching in her driveway. She said, *I know this nigger didn't come to my house unannounced without calling. He must want me to put two hollow points in his head.* Wallace jumped out his car and grabbed Angel by her arm and pulled her back into the house, making her almost drop her daughter that sent Angel into a rage that Wallace wasn't ready for. When Angel put her daughter down, she lost it. She went into her kitchen, picked up a butcher knife, and started sticking Wallace so fast he hit the floor. When she bent down, she was still sticking him with the knife. She didn't stop until he didn't have a breath in his body.

She looked at Wallace and said, "Nigger, don't nobody mess with my daughter, and I should have told you, sucker, I'm killer,." Angel said, *Damn, now I got to bury this fool,* so she took a big piece of plastic, wrapped him up in it, and dragged him to her car to put in her trunk. She knew of a spot to take him to. It was a small lot behind a building she past by one day. They had equipment setup to pouring concrete, so she said, *It would be a good place because they won't smell his ass when he starts stinking.*

After Angel buried Wallace in the cement grave, she left with a smile on her face, feeling good, because she had another notch on her belt. She was on her way to get some food when her phone rang again. It was Uncle Leo. He had an assignment for her; she was to get home to get the information he had delivered to her house while she was out. He had pictures of the guy he wanted Angel to kill. He owed two hundred thousand dollars to the family. He knew they were looking for him, so he skipped out of town.

Angel got home and saw the envelope slid under her front door. She put her daughter to bed, got her a drink, and started to look in the envelope to see who this person was. When she saw the man's picture that she had to kill, she said, *Oh my god,* she said to herself, *I would have done this one for free.* The picture she saw was Judge Baker's. She said, *I'm going back to Chicago quicker than I thought so I might as well kill two birds with one stone.*

Angel was geared up to go back to Chicago. She was already going to Chicago the weekend anyway. She had Judge Baker in mind as her next victim. She went to Chicago that Friday. She went to her loft and took a shower and headed for Club Sexy. When she made it there, the club was jumping. She spotted Judge Baker sitting in his favored spot, so she made her way over to his table because she knew he liked attractive woman to do freaky things to him, so she had that part covered.

She asked him, "Do you want to go upstairs to VIP with me?"

He said, "Yes. Is there a room up there with a door?"

She said, "Of course, it is handsome. Are you ready to go?"

The Judge jumped up and headed to the stairs.

Angel said, "This is going to be too damn easy."

When Angel and the judge made it upstairs, she asked the judge, "What is it you want me to do for you, handsome?"

He told Angel, "I want you to take my belt off and spank me with it."

She said, "Is there anything else you prefer me to do?"

He said, "Yes, I want you to take the heel of your shoe and step on my balls with them, and then I want you to take this, candle and light it, and pour the hot wax down the crack of my ass."

Angel said, "Oh yes, I can do that."

Angel left the room and went to the restroom. She had her pistol strapped to her thigh, and she wanted the judge to remember her as Angel Carter.

She asked the judge, "Can I get down and freak with you?"

He told Angel, "Come on with it. I can handle whatever you throw at me."

That was right up Angel's alley. She came equipped with guns, switchblades, duct tape, and she had battery acid in a jar in her purse. She was going to make this judge pay for sending her away to that hellhole of a prison.

Angel gave the judge a drink that she spiked. He started slurring; she knew then he was up for the taking, so she laid him back on the bed and took her switchblade and cut off his eyelids so he couldn't shut his eyes. She wanted the judge to see everything she was going to do to him. She said, "You don't remember me, do you? I'm Angel Carter, the one you said was a threat to the city of Chicago."

The judge couldn't do nothing but jump around on the bed because Angel had him tied down with duct tape; he knew she was going to kill him.

Angel said, "Your Honor, I'm going to make this very quick. Don't worry, the pain is going to be like snatching off a bandage. You are going to die fast."

She loaded up a needle with some liquid Amtrak and gave the judge a big dose, and he swelled up like a basketball instantly. Angel left the room and never looked back. She had one more victim to get rid of before she left Chicago on Sunday. She went to meet up with the next judge on her hit list, Judge O'Malley.

Angel made a call to Judge O'Malley to come meet her at the Motel 6. She said she was a call girl that needed his attention. O'Malley said, "How do I know you and where did you get my number?"

She said, "From the agency you use to get private shows." He told her, "I know what you talking about. I'll be there around eight. I will be here in room

312 on the third floor. Who should I ask for Crystal? All right, Crystal, I see you then."

When Judge O'Malley made it to the room, he was disappointed because he never been in a dump of a hotel before. He had always been to the Hilton or the Marriott, so this was a step down for him, but he was there, and he was going to get his freak on and go home to his wife, but what he didn't know he would never see Mrs. O'Malley again.

Angel asked Judge O' Malley, "What is your specialty of the night?"

He told Angel, "I want a bathtub full of Jell-O and a spoon so I could eat some while I'm relaxing. Once he got out the tub, I want you to spread some whip cream on genitals and lick them slowly."

Angel said, "All right, Your Honor, if that's what you want, then your wish is my command."

Angel told the judge she had to go in the bedroom for a minute she had a gift for him in her purse. When Angel came back from the bedroom, she had a blow torch. The judge looked up at Angel like he had just been hit by lightening.

She said, "Judge O'Malley, this is your chance to say a prayer for your forgiveness. You need to hurry because you don't have that much time."

The judge was in tears. He said, "Please don't kill me. I have a wife and three children."

Angel said, "That's funny because if your wife meant that much to you, your freaky ass wouldn't be here sitting in a bathtub of Jell-O fend to get fried with a blow torch."

That scared the judge even more because Angel lit up the blow torch and aimed it right at the judge. His skin was frying from that blow torch like chicken in hot grease.

Angel left the hotel satisfied she had killed two birds with one stone. She headed back to her loft on the outskirts of Chicago and took a shower and went to bed. The next morning, she got up and hit the highway on her way back to California. She would come back to Chicago later to finish what she started. She had an army of people there she still had on her hit list. Angel made it back from Chicago only to find another envelope under her door. She looked at it and threw it on the table.

Angel couldn't sleep that night, so she got up, went and got the envelope off the table, and opened it up. She saw two pictures of two Russian guys: one of them was Boris, the head of the Russian mafia; the second one was Boris's brother, the second guy in command. Uncle Leo wanted the Russian mafia out of his way; they kept interfering with his shipment's he had trucks going through Russia, and they would kill every man that was from Columbia.

Ramon sent Angel a passport. She had all the information she needed to set up camp in Russia. She just needed someone to keep her daughter; there was no way she was taking her daughter to Russia. Ramon had Angel's back. He sent Mary, their housekeeper, to watch Angel's daughter while she was gone to Russia. Angel trusted Mary because she spent a lot of time with her Baby Girl when they were in Columbia. Now that Mary had made it to California, it was time for Angel to take flight and bounce to Russia.

Ramon had set Angel up in a nice village in Russia; he also made sure she had all the artillery she needed. Angel had missiles, hand grenades, guns, and even had C4, so she was ready to blow up Russia if she had to. Angel moved in the night like a ninja. She was so light on her feet that she was confident that she wouldn't get detected. Angel stayed in her room during the day, and at night, she would go and plant C4 around the Russian compound. She wanted to make sure the whole Russian mafia family was destroyed.

Angel planted herself a dirt hole she made outside of the compound. She had all the artillery in the hole with her. That way if anybody came out of the compound when she blew it up, they was going to get hit with her AK-47s or hand grenades. She even had two meat cleavers. Angel was going to slice and dice. She was going to do whatever it took to get the job done so she could get the hell out of Russia.

That night Angel lit the compound up like it was the Fourth of July. It was raining people; they were trying to escape the fire, but Angel wasn't letting anyone escape when she came up out of that dirt hole. It was four guys running out of the compound. She took her meat clever and cut their heads clean off their shoulders. They didn't even see it coming because they were running with their bodies on fire.

Angel's job was done in Russia. She got herself together and headed back to the airport, but when she got to the airport, she couldn't leave. The Russian police had the airport and everything locked down so that no one was leaving Russia. So she had to go to plan B. She called Ramon and told him the job was done, but there was no way she was leaving Russia by plane. She told him she set off such an explosion that half of Russia was gone.

Ramon told his pilot to fuel up they were going to Russia to pick up Angel. Uncle Leo told them to be careful and to fly under the radar. Angel knew to meet Ramon and the pilot on high ground. She had to get on the high end of Russia to get picked up, so she knew where to go. She left the airport soon. Ramon told her he was on his way. They picked Angel up eight hours later, and she was on her way home without a scratch and two million dollars richer.

Chapter Twenty-Three
Angel s Killing Spree in Chicago

ANGEL WAS GLAD to be out of Russia; she had wiped out another mafia family; she was back home with her daughter she was going to rest up a while before she headed back to the Windy City. She was watching the news. When she saw this dark-skinned woman crying, she said her husband had been missing for two months; the lady gave a description of her husband, and she also had a photo of him. When Angel saw the photo, she said to herself, *Lady, you will never see that lying son of bitch husband of yours again. I buried your husband Wallace in a concrete grave two months ago.*

Angel was at home sitting around, and she started to get a little uneasy she wanted more blood spilled, so she thought it was a good time to take a trip back to Chicago. Angel entered Chicago and went straight to her restaurant. The Sugar Shack she was sitting there eating when she saw two of her soldiers. Angel's soldiers had dismantled when Angel went to jail, so she had no intentions on regrouping her soldiers. She was a one woman-killing machine on her own, so she didn't need backup.

When Angel sat down at a table behind them, she heard Mia's name come up, so she really wanted to know what they were saying. When she heard them say Mia was looking for Angel to kill her for smoking her brother St. Louis, she knew then to add Mia's name to her hit list.

Angel knew she came there to kill Hammer first, her brother's right-hand man, because he sat there on the witness stand at her trail and said he was put into their organization as an informant for the police department. She wanted his head for sure; he wasn't going to get away that easy. Angel knew just where to find Hammer by him being retired. It was a cakewalk for her because she heard he was hanging out at a bar they called Thigh High. *Were the women there had big thighs?* When Angel walked in, she had every guy there whispering about who she was, so she didn't make it difficult for them to find out who she was. She ordered rounds for everybody in the club, including the women. She made sure the bartender kept them coming. She wanted everybody in the club stupid drunk because she didn't want anyone to remember her snatching Hammer's big ass up out of the club.

Angel waited until Hammer past out in the booth. He was sitting in; she woke him up and asked him if he wanted to go have some fun with her. She even let him rub her ass. Hammer looked at Angel and said, "You, damn skippy, I want to have some fun with you. My truck is parked out back. We can do whatever you want to do in my truck. My seats lay all the way back, plus I have tinted windows so no one can see inside my truck. So, come on, Baby Girl, we going to go burn some rubber."

Angel waited until she got Hammer undressed inside his truck, and she covered his eyes with a scarf. She proceeded to use her handcuffs to handcuff him to the steering wheel of his truck. After he was handcuffed, she took his blackjack and started beating Hammer to death with his own nightstick. She told Hammer, "This is what you get for being a snitch and a trader."

Hammer was so out of it he couldn't comprehend nothing Angel was saying. She beat Hammer so bad in the head until his eyeballs popped out of his head and his nose was on the left side of his face. He was going to have a closed casket funeral because his face and head was disfigured completely.

Angel wasn't finished yet; she was on to her next victim, the police commissioner. He came to her cell while she was in locked up in the back waiting to be transported to the women's prison; he tried to rape her. If it wasn't for the female sheriff, he would have raped her for sure. She came in and called Angel's name right on time. The commissioner looked at Angel and said, "Next time we will be alone and I'm going to rip you another asshole. You can believe that, Ms. Carter."

Angel couldn't shake what the commissioner said to her that day. She kept playing what he said over and over in her head like it was a scratched CD, but she had to make him pay for being so damn stupid. She thought to herself, *How you going to try to rape a prisoner while she's waiting to be transported to another jail.* She knew he was a sick man, but she was going to make sure his sickness never reached another female on lockdown.

Angel was sitting in her car at a red light when the commissioner pulled up right beside her. She said to herself, *All hell. This must be my lucky day. This asshole is about to meet his maker sooner than I thought.* Angel let the commissioner pull off first so she could follow him to wherever he was going. When she saw him pull up to this house on her old street and Mia came to the door wrapped in a towel, she said, *Yes, this is my lucky day, because I don't have to go looking for this bitch she right where she needs to be.* Angel decided to go around to the back of the house so she could break out the basement window and slid on in. When she hit the basement floor, she landed on top of a pile of dirt clothes. She stopped for a minute and laughed to herself because Mia was a trifling female.

Angel was creeping up the basement stairs when she heard some screaming. She peeped through the crack she had in the door when she saw the commissioner chocking the dog shit out of Mia. Angel said in her mind, *Kill the bitch, and once you done with her, it's your turn, you crazy ass pervert.* The commissioner stopped chocking Mia because he heard something. He let Mia go, and she dropped to the floor like an old rag doll. He went to the kitchen because he thought the sound came out of there. When he turned around to go back in there to chock Mia, Angel came out from behind the basement door with a bat she found in the basement and hit the commissioner upside the head and knocked him buck out.

When the commissioner came too, he was tied to Mia's bed right beside her on her bed. Angel slapped Mia to wake her up so she would know the reason Angel was killing her. Angel told Mia and the commissioner that they wouldn't live to see daylight. Mia was squirming, trying to get loose when Angel said, "You might as well be still because when Angel Carter tie a knot, you can't take it a loose."

The commissioner looked at angel to see if she really was Angel Carter, but he couldn't see the resemblance because Angel had plastic surgery done on her face, plus she had contacts in her eyes and had changed her hair color and everything.

Angel asked the commissioner, "Do you know the game operation dumb ass?"

He said, "Yeah."

Angel said, "Good, because I'm going to operate on both of y'all."

When she said that, Mia started screaming so loud that Angel put a sock in her mouth and taped her mouth shut. Angel told the commissioner, "I think I'm going to start with you first." She put her purse on the bed and pulled out a machete.

She hit the commissioner right down the middle of his chest with it and took out his heart and put it in a plastic bag. Next, Angel started on Mia. She told Mia, "I always loved the color of your eyes. I think I will take your eyeballs out and mail them to your son that you didn't think I knew about, huh? Your son name is Shawn, isn't it?"

She said, "Yes, but please don't put my son through that kind of trauma. Angel, please. He doesn't have anything to do with this."

Angel said, "You should have thought about your son being traumatized when you decided to cross me, but you know I will give you the honor of calling your son one last time before I put you to sleep."

Angel gave Mia the phone to call her son. She was crying, and her twelve-year-old son asked her, "Why are you crying?"

She said, "Because I love you, and I always will."

Angel motioned for Mia to hang up the phone, and she told her son goodnight, which will be the last time he would hear his mother's voice. Angel wind up electrocuting Mia, and once Mia took her last breath, Angel cut Mia's eyeballs out and put them in a plastic bag with the commissioner's heart.

When Angel was about to leave Mia's house, she thought to herself, *I just couldn't leave their bodies lying out like that.* So she went in the garage, got the gas can, poured gas all through the house, and set the house on fire. She went back out Mia's house the same way she came in through the basement window.

Angel liked the way blood felt on her hands every time she killed someone. She felt a burst of energy. It made her heart pump extra hard. She liked the excitement it gave her. She finished her job in Chicago. Everyone that was involved in her case was now dead. In her heart, she knew she had two more people to destroy, but she wanted to just sit back and let nature take its course on those two because she knew her two friends Abby and Gabriel would be waiting on her arrival. So Angel decided to let them watch their backs for a while because when she came for them in the shadows of the night, they won't even know she's there.

Chapter Twenty-Four
Angel: The One Woman-Killing Machine

ANGEL WAS IN Columbia on an assignment. This time, she was there for three weeks. She had to go to Delaware to meet a guy name Paul Adams. He was supposed to be running that part of town for the Columbians. When Angel arrived in Delaware, she checked into the Holiday Inn. She had two days to connect with Paul. He owned a bar called The Vault. It was the hottest club in the Delaware area. Paul had pole dancers, strippers, and even had rooms in the back where they had orgies with mixed couples. He had bodyguards at each door.

Paul used to be a pimp; he dressed like he was still in the seventies. He thought that he was every woman's dream and every man's nightmare. He had enough jewelry on his hands to choke a horse. He treated his women like they were God's gift for men. He hated the Columbians. He thought that if he took their money and skipped town, they would send their men after him, and when they came for him, he would be ready. But what Paul didn't know was they were sending someone for him, but it was what he loved the most is what's gone take his ass out of here.

Angel rented her a Rolls-Royce with a GPS on it so she knew actually where Club Vault was located. When she stepped through the doors, she had all eyes on her. She was dressed in an all-white leather dress with the back cut out all the way down to ass. She had the white Armani and white boots to match; she had two pearl-white forty-fives attached to her side under her white fur coat. She was ready for whatever jumped off. Angel went to the bar to order her a cognac with a water back. She wanted to get a feel of Club Vault. She even went to the restroom a couple of times to look for escape routes. She didn't even worry about Paul's bodyguards. She had them eating out the palm of her hands like little puppies.

Angel had been sitting in Club Vault for an hour, and she still hadn't spotted Paul yet; she knew what he looked like because she had a picture of him. Another hour later and two more cognacs later, Paul came in the door, sporting a white mink coat with two white chicks on his arm. Angel was damn near drunk because she thought Paul's ugly ass was fine. She said to herself, *Shake this shit off because there's my victim right there, so let me get to work.*

Angel got up to go to the restroom again while Paul was standing at the bar. She knew he peeped her when he came in the door, so she knew by her making eye contact with him, he was going to want to know who she was. Paul asked his bartender what was she drinking and to give her another one on him. When Angel came back to the bar where she was sitting, the bartender handed her another drink. Angel said, "Excuse me, I didn't order another drink."

The bartender pointed down to the end of the bar where Paul was standing, holding up his drink. He was looking up at Angel and waving his hand for Angel to come and join him.

Angel got up and went to the end of the bar where Paul was. He pulled out the bar stool for Angel to sit down. Paul extended his hand out to introduce himself to Angel. She told him her name was Jennifer. He told Angel that's a beautiful name for a beautiful woman. Angel said thank you. They had two more drinks together before Paul invited Angel upstairs to his office. Angel didn't mind going to Paul's office because she could take his life anywhere.

Paul and Angel were sitting in his office when he told Angel he had to go drain the dragon. She said "sure, go ahead."

While Paul was out of the office, Angel took her guns off and put them behind her back so Paul couldn't see them. He was so drunk he couldn't have seen a snake if it was crawling across the floor. The music was pumping so loud no one was going to hear Angel's forty-fives going off. She had silencers on both of them. She even had hollow point bullets in them.

Paul got straight to the point with Angel. He told Angel, "Damn, baby, I want to see what you working with under that coat."

She told Paul, "Only if you let me see what you working with in your pants."

He said, "I'm working with a monster. Baby, you might not be able to handle all this."

Angel said, "Pull it out for me, daddy. Let me see this monster."

Paul took his pants off, and lo and behold, his dick was so long and thick it hit the floor. Angel said damn.

Angel's job was to kill the man, but when she saw Paul's meat, she wanted some of that, so she sat on Paul's lap and rode him like a bronco bull. Paul told Angel that was the best piece of ass he had in a long time. He was so worn out that Angel got down off his lap and took her forty-five and stuck it in his mouth and said, "Never trust a bitch with a gun." Angel also told Paul that she was a Columbian assassin sent by Leo to kill him, and his time on this earth had just been deleted.

Angel was on her way down the steps when one of Paul's bodyguards asked her was Paul still in his office. She told him that he was but he was in his restroom washing up. "Give him a minute and he would be right down."

She went to the bar for a minute before she went out the door. She didn't get a chance to make it to the door before the bodyguard shouted, "Hold that bitch." Before the other bodyguard could get close to Angel, she swung back her coat and came up with her twins, the forty-fives were blazing. She had hit about twenty people before she stopped shooting. Angel didn't get hit at all because the bodyguards didn't even have a chance to pull their weapons out. Angel was ruthless when it came to pistol play; she had Club Vault smoking.

Angel checked out the Holiday Inn that night. She kept the car she rented. She decided to roll the Rolls-Royce to another town and turn it in there. She didn't think she could go in as quickly as she did to kill Paul, but she did know that men weren't going to turn down known ass, that's where he fucked up at. He should have kept it moving, but no, he want to stick his dick in something hot and look where it got him dead.

Angel arrived back in Columbia in record time. She had completed another hit. She was glad to be back to see her Baby Girl laugh. She was in the room with her daughter when Uncle Leo knocked on her door.

She said, "Come in."

Uncle Leo came in and gave Angel five hundred thousand dollars for the job she had just completed. He gave Angel another envelope with pictures of three men he wanted her to kill. She looked at Uncle Leo and said, "When do I leave?"

He said, "At dawn."

She told Uncle Leo, "I will be ready. I just need to go to the gun house to choose some more artillery to take with me. I'm going to need some C4 too. This time, they won't remember what hit them."

Angel had Uncle Leo to have the jet fueled up. She was on her way to Fresno, California. She had three hits to carry out. They were the head of the Crips and Bloods. She had enough ammunition with her to blow up Fresno. She even took a powerful stun gun with her too because she wanted to make a statement to make sure the guys on the West Coast felt the pressure she was tend to put on their assess. Angel felt uneasy about this trip. She didn't feel like she normally does, but she just said to herself, *It would be fine.*

Angel arrived in Fresno, California, and checked into the Sheraton Hotel. She went to the car rental and rented a 2011 pearl-white Bentley. She drove through Fresno, bumping her music to Gerald Levert's "School Me" from his private-label CD. She turned on her GPS to get the location of where the Crips and Bloods spot was on Imperial Street. She had her mind made up to hit their spot as soon as it got dark. She drove down Imperial Street and spotted her three targets. They were heavily guarded, so she said to herself, *I'm not going to be wasting my time. Everyone in the house has to go.*

Angel had pictures of all three of her targets: Ace, Casper, and Buck were the heads of their organization. They had hits on them for killing Uncle Leo's son that was visiting his girlfriend in Fresno. She used to mess around with Ace. When Ace came over to Anita's house one night, Leo's son Rickey was there. They got into a gunfight, and Rickey was hit twice in the head and died right on the spot. Ace sent Rickey back to Columbia in a wooden box. Uncle Leo took that as a threat to the Columbians, so Ace and his whole organization had to be deleted.

Angel had time on hands until it got dark, so she pulled up to a restaurant to get her something to eat. She put in her order. She was sitting at her table texting Ramon when she heard some guys arguing with each other. She stop texting and looked up, and it was all three of her targets, and at least six more guys with them. She said to herself, *Either these niggers are following me or maybe I'm just tripping. I think I'm going with the tripping part because they can't possibly think I'm here to kill them.*

Angel received her food, but she kept feeling someone staring at her, so she looked up and it was Casper. He came over to her table and asked Angel, "Can I sit down?"

She said, "Yes, it's a free country."

Casper said, "What's your name, beautiful?"

Angel said, "What's yours? You came over here interrupting my meal."

He said, "My name is Casper."

Angel said, "Like Casper the Friendly Ghost?"

He said, "Yeah, something like that."

She laughed, "All right, Casper the Friendly Ghost, my name is Jenny like I dream of Jennie."

"Oh, I see, you got jokes, all right. I like that you're not from around here."

Angel said, "How do you know that?"

Casper told Angel, "I run Fresno. I know everyone here, and there's no way I would have missed someone as fine as you are."

"Well, you missed me, player. I've been around for a while."

"Oh, really, okay. Why is it that I haven't just seen you then, because I didn't want to be seen?"

Angel wasn't trying to get picked up by Casper and no one else in his crew. She was going to set fire to their assess and bounce back to Columbia soon as it darkens enough for her to do her job. She didn't even like his conversation. It really was a hit-and-miss with her. Everything he said went over her head because she really wasn't interested.

Casper said, "Damn, ma, I never had a female to give me such a cold shoulder. You do like men, don't you, ma?"

"Of course, I love men. You just isn't the type of man I go for."

"Damn, ma, that was cold."

"No disrespect. I like men that wear belts to keep their pants up, not with their pants down to their ankles."

"All right, I feel you. So in other words, you telling me if I put a belt on and pull my pants up, I might have a shot with you?"

"Know what I'm saying is I like a man with class, that's all. Let me wrap this up real quick for you. I'm not interested in you, period."

Angel left the restaurant and didn't look back, but she still had Casper's attention. He couldn't let go the feeling that Angel shut him down. That has never happened to him before, so he was angry at the fact that his boys were teasing him about a girl that was fine like Angel doesn't want no parts of Casper.

Angel made Casper second-guess himself because he was the finest one out of his whole crew. He had never been dismissed by female before. Casper told his crewman, "Something has to be wrong with that bitch. Don't know female pass up a nigger like me. She must like pussy for real dog. Look, check this out. We gone forget about what just happened and stick to the job at hand. We are going to roll on these fools on the West Side. We know where their meth lab is. We go in there and take their shit and roll out."

Buck said, "Hold up, Casper. You talking crazy because them boys got some mad-fire powered up in there, so do we fool. Stop being a bitch and let's go. How about you, Ace? You ready or you tripping out too?"

"No, I'm down for whatever man, so let's make it do what it does."

Angel stayed on the parking lot watching them fools every move. They were so much into what they were doing they didn't even notice Angel following close behind them. They all put their masks on and kicked the front door open to the meth lab and went in. Angel sat across the street watching the whole thing take place. She said, *These niggers are gangsters but not gangster enough, because they are going to be deleted by a real gangster—me. As soon as the sun goes down, I'm going to put their lights out.*

Angel went back to Sheraton to get her artillery, put it in duffel bag, and headed back out the door. She had everything from switchblades to oozies. She brought C4 for emergency backup. She went back to Imperial Street and sat there until it got dark, but she sat further down the street this time since they saw what she was driving. Angel's mind was working overtime. She thought, *I need to take this car back to the hotel and park it and steal me a beat-up ride that's dark in color.* Angel took the car back to the hotel, parked it, and stole a car off the hotel parking lot. The car she stole was a black Impala. She thought, *It wouldn't get noticed as much as the pearl-white Bentley.*

Angel went back to Imperial Street and sat down the street, she even scooted down in the seat so no one would notice a suspicious woman sitting in a car. It got dark quick. Angel put her artillery in the front seat so she could take out what she needed to blow the house up with while she was in the duffel bag taking out what she needed. She saw two little boys go in the house. She said to herself, *Damn! I hope they go in and come out because I would hate to blow their little assess up in smoke with the rest of them clowns. If I'm going to give them twenty minutes, after that it's smoking time.*

Angel waited twenty minutes as promised. They didn't come out, so she had to do what she was sent there to do, under different circumstances. If it was a job that she was doing on her own, she would have given the little boys more time to come out, but this wasn't a job for herself. This was about money, and nothing or no one was going to stop her from getting her paper. Angel took two packages of the C4 she had in her bag, plus two oozies. She strapped two thirty-eight snug nose pistols on her side.

Angel snuck up to the house crawling on her stomach. She put C4 around the house. She set the detonators and jumped in the bushes to hide. She was waiting for anybody that came out the house alive when she fired up the detonators, all hell broke loose. The house sounded off with a big boom. She could see bodies flying through the air. When she came up out the bushes, she was standing face-to-face with Casper. Angel pulled the oozies out and fired so many rounds through Casper's body. He looked like chopped up beef. He looked at Angel and dropped in the grass. He was dead before he hit the grass. The whole gang (organization) had been deleted—another assignment completed.

Angel was on her way home from Fresno when the thought of her being a mother hit her like a bolt of lightning. She has no family left; she only has her daughter. Angel had a premonition about her daughter growing up without the love and affection of her mother. Angel was so caught up in being an assassin that she had forgotten about the love that bonds a mother and daughter together. Her first instinct was to cut her job as an assassin to a minimal. She would only go out on an assignment once a month. She was going to tell Uncle Leo about her agreement, and if he doesn't accept her terms, she would have to decline rights of being their personal assassin.

Angel took her concerns to Uncle Leo and the other Columbian members, and they totally agreed that as good as Angel was as their assassin, she had all rights to spend time raising her daughter. They knew how important family was. Angel took her daughter back to California to start her mother and daughter relationship. She had plans on raising her daughter the way she was raised. She wanted to train Gloria to be a trained assassin as well. Angel wanted her Baby Girl fifteen years later to be said as mother and daughter assassins for the Columbian mafia.

Chapter Twenty-Five
Baby Girl in Training

ANGEL GOT UP early this morning taking her Baby Girl to her first training at the shooting range. Gloria was excited to go. She had been begging Angel for weeks when will it be her turn to hold a gun. Angel made sure she explained how serious guns were. She wanted her daughter to know every aspects of being an assassin. She had to start from the bottom up like she was taught. Angel took her Baby Girl through a two-year military training, which was hard on Baby Girl. But she wanted it all; she wanted to be her mother's shadow.

Angel even went as far as putting her daughter in military camouflage to let her know that being assassin is a serious business and just one slip up could get them killed. Angel made Baby Girl go to one year of mixed martial arts training before she decided to take her out on a job to watch her back. Angel was sent on an assignment to St. Louis to hit this drug lord by name black a.k.a. Danny Stone. He ran the West Side of the city of St. Louis. He ran his operation all the way to the Central West End.

Black was getting his drugs from the Columbians, and he was short changing them with fake money. His last shipment was fifty thousand dollars of pure uncut heroin. He sent his right-hand man, The Sandman, to Columbia to pick up the package. The Sandman gave the Columbians the money and headed back to St. Louis. When the Columbians realized they had been played with phony money, they were pissed. They knew Black needed to be dealt with. The Columbians put a call in to their personal assassin, Angel.

Angel was more than happy to get an assignment because she was taking her Baby Girl with her as backup. This was her first time out the gate and Angel wanted her ready. Angel and Baby Girl made it to St. Louis that morning. They checked in to the Hyatt Hotel in downtown St. Louis. She got in her car and turned on her GPS to locate the West Side of St. Louis to find a street called Blackstone. Twenty minutes later, Angel was pulling up on Blackstone Street. She sat on the corner of Blackstone and Page Avenues mapping out her escape routes.

Angel and Baby Girl were sitting in her car watching traffic coming and going out of Black's drug house. She had pictures of Black, but she had yet to see the head nigger in charge. Baby Girl started getting hungry, so she asked Angel how long were they going to sit out there before she got something to eat. Angel said, "Listen to me carefully. When you stalking a target, you never leave your post unless it's daylight like it is now, or you got him in focus in your eyesight so you can take him out right then."

Angel's Baby Girl understood what Angel was saying, and she decided she could eat later because after they hit Black, they would be on their way back to California. Angel and Baby Girl were still sitting on the corner watching Black's spot in a black tricked out charger with tinted windows didn't sit well with one of black soldiers. He spotted them after about twenty minutes of sitting there. He gave Black a call to let him know that they were either being watched by the police or some niggers who wanted to rob his spot.

Black was at his apartment when Blaze called, so he told his soldier Blaze to get two more of his soldiers and run up on the side of Angel's car and snatch them up out their ride and take them in the dope house and hold them there until he arrives. Black said, "No better yet. Let's hold out until it gets dark. You know, we got people already watching our block, just chill for now. It'll be dark in an hour, so just be cool until then."

Angel started to feel like somebody was watching her, so she decided to leave her post. She wanted to change cars. Something told Angel that she had already been pepped. Angel went to steal a Buick. She wanted a car that they haven't noticed sitting outside the dope house. Black called Blaze to see if the car was still there. Blaze answered on the first ring. He told Black the car was gone.

Black told Blaze to pack up everything and move it down to their other dope house on Wells and he would meet him there in a half-hour. Blaze said, "Cool, I'll see you then." Black started sweating. He said to himself, *Something isn't right. Maybe those punk-ass Russians sent somebody to hit my ass or it might be that nigger Bo Pete we robbed last week and took all his shit, including the nigger's safe. That nigger Bo Pete is scary he don't have the balls to try and come at me because he know what time it is.*

Angel followed Blaze to the dope house on Wells. He was so busy moving dope around he didn't notice the Buick following him. Angel and Baby Girl had their artillery ready for what was about to jump off. Angel had two MAC-10s, four oozies, and some hand grenades. What Angel saw next put the icing on the cake. It was her target Black. He pulled up driving a burgundy Yukon.

Angel told her daughter, "There he is, right there. This is going to be short and sweet. We will be back home before the sun comes up." Angel told her daughter to put on her camouflage uniform because it was going to be dark in a few minutes, and they were going in blazing. She didn't want to leave a soul alive left in that house. Angel took all the artillery out the bag. She started strapping the MAC-10s to her thigh. She gave Baby Girl two oozies and two switchblades. Baby Girl was excited to be on her first assignment with her mother.

Angel told Baby Girl that she was going in through the front door and wanted her outside the back door hiding in the bushes. She wanted Baby Girl in the bushes firing at anyone that comes out the back door. Angel kicked in the front door, shooting. She hit Blaze so many times with the MAC-10 until he hit the floor like a ton of bricks.

Angel ripped the other four guys that were in the house to shreds. They were so high off heroin they didn't even hear the door being kicked in. Black tried to escape through the back door when Baby Girl shot him twice in the leg. He dropped to the ground holding his leg. She was under instructions from Angel not to kill him, so she thought that by shooting him in the leg that would slow him down.

While Angel was in the house, she heard the gunshots coming from the back of the house, so she ran to the back to see was Baby Girl all right. When she saw that Baby Girl had Black pinned down she smiled because Baby Girl had paid attention to her training. Angel told Black that she was going to take him for a little ride. He was bleeding badly from his leg. Angel had a syringe loaded with heroin to put Black to sleep until she got to her next destination.

Angel found a vacant storefront building empty on Page Boulevard. She got out the car with her Baby Girl and dragged Black inside the vacant storefront. He was still blazing off that heroin Angel stuck in his neck. Angel told Black to wake up and pay attention because she was only going to say it once. Angel had Baby Girl to go to the car and get her battery-operated saw. She was going to make sure Black never gave anyone phony money again because his number was up.

Angel asked Black, "Why would you think that the Columbians would be so stupid and not have their money checked?"

Black said, "Fuck the Columbians bitch and fuck you too."

Angel said, "All right, let's see who gets fucked now, player."

Angel started up her battery-operated saw, and she took both of Black's legs off first. He was screaming so loud that this homeless man woke up from his sleep; he was in the back of the store, sleeping.

Angel had Baby Girl watching the front of the empty store to make sure if anybody past by she could let her know. The homeless man peeped through a hole in the wall and saw Angel cutting Black up with a saw. He got so scared until he pissed in his pants. The homeless man, Dirty Bob, jumped back so far that he knocked over a can. Angel heard the noise. She went to investigate what she heard and Dirty Bob was frozen stiff with fear. Before Angel could ask him what he saw, he told Angel, "I didn't see anything and I don't know anything."

Angel said, "I'm sorry, but I don't leave witnesses."

Dirty Bob told Angel, "I am already homeless and didn't have anything. The least you can do is let me live."

Angel apologized again to Dirty Bob. He just happened to be at the wrong place at wrong time. Angel pulled out one of her MAC-10s. She shot Dirty Bob twice in the forehead. Dirty Bob fell backward with his eyes wide open. Baby Girl heard the shots. She went in the vacant store to make sure everything was okay. When she saw Dirty Bob on the floor dead with eyes wide open, she said, "What the hell." She asked Angel, "Where did he come from."

She told Baby Girl, "He was hiding in the back room. I thought I told you to check out the back of the store."

Baby Girl knew she checked out the back of the store to make sure she wasn't second-guessing herself. She went back to the room in the back of the store and looked in a corner in the room where it was a pile of cardboard boxes. That's where Dirty Bob was hiding because the boxes had been moved a little to the side of the room. Angel and Baby Girl jumped in the car to go to the service station to get some gas. Angel got the gas, went back to the vacant store, and poured gasoline all through the store. Baby Girl lit a match and threw it on the cardboard boxes. Angel and Baby Girl left the storefront and didn't look back.

Angel and Baby Girl went back to the hotel; she checked out. They were going to Red Lobster to get something to eat before they left St. Louis. When they were parking on the parking lot at Red Lobster, they saw a guy that could be identical to Black, so they had to think of something quick to find out who this guy was that was going into Red Lobster. He looked just like the man they just killed. Angel told Baby Girl, "This is how we are going to play this out when we get inside the restaurant. I'm going to drop my purse. I'm going to bend over right in front of him so he could get a peek at my fat ass."

Angel's plan went off without a hitch just like she thought. She dropped her purse to make sure she left her lipstick on the floor so he could bring it to their table as planned. When Black's twin brother Smokey came over to the table, Angel and Baby Girl were in shock: they were identical. To find out more information, Angel invited him to have lunch with her and Baby Girl.

Smokey told Angel, "Hold up a minute, ma. I have guest coming to join me. Is it all right if we all join you at your table?"

Angel said, "If it's all right with my sister, it's all right with me."

Baby Girl knew what Angel was talking about, so she followed her suit and said, "Sure, it's fine. Go get your crew so we can put our order in."

Smokey came back to the table with three of his soldiers. He was sitting beside Angel fantasizing about getting a room and clamming between Angel's legs.

Angel's mind was somewhere else. She was just hoping she hadn't killed the wrong guy, but in reality, she didn't care because killing was her job but mistakes didn't have any room in her business. Once everyone came back to Angel's table, they introduced themselves. Angel said her name was Nicole and Baby Girl told them her name was Penny. Smokey said, "My name is Black. I have a twin brother by name Smokey. We just switched places for the day to send the police in a different direction."

Then Black introduced his three soldiers to Angel as Blocker, Hot Head, and Cricket. Angel and Baby Girl said in unison, "Nice to meet you," and excused their selves for a bathroom break.

When Angel and Baby Girl went to the restroom, they came up with a plan to get another hotel room and take their company with them. Angel saw how Black kept looking at her behind, so she knew she could get him to follow her to the hotel. When they all were done eating, Black asked Angel, "What are you about to get into?"

Angel told Black, "You know how Black's folks are after they eat they be ready to go to sleep, so that's what I'm getting ready to do. I'm getting me a room and get some sleep for a couple of hours."

Black told Angel, "I hear you, ma. I just wish I could keep you company while you sleep, that's all."

"Well," Angel said, "let me get my room first. Maybe I might let you keep me company for a little while."

Angel knew she was going to call Black because her mission to kill him wasn't completed. So after she and Baby Girl got to the hotel, they got two rooms that joined together. Black wasn't going by himself. Since it was two of them, he asked Angel if he could bring Cricket with him. She said sure. She knew Cricket wasn't going to be a problem. He stood five foot two and weighed a hundred pounds. She knew Baby Girl could break his neck easily.

Angel and Baby Girl got in the car and drove to the Pear Tree Hotel. They made reservations on the phone. When they got there, their rooms were ready. Angel had piano string ready with a forty-four that she called Pistol Pete. She made sure Baby Girl had her weapon of choice too. Baby Girl wanted the forty-five. Angel kept it in the glove compartment of the car, so she went and got it out the car. Baby Girl also wanted the two switchblades.

They stayed in Angel's room for two hours before they decided to call Black and Cricket to come to their rooms. Angel ordered some wine from room service and spiked it she had enough LSD in the wine to knock them out cold. Right after room service bought the wine to the room, Angel spiked it. Black started knocking on the door. He had changed clothes, and everything Angel said to herself, *It doesn't even matter because this nigger here won't make it out this room alive.*

Angel and Baby Girl had music going in both rooms, plus they had two bottles of wine set to the side for themselves so they won't drink out the spiked bottle of wine, Black and Cricket started feeling real good. They wanted to slow dance with Angel and Baby Girl. Angel took Black by the hand, pulled him up off the bed, and started dancing. Baby Girl followed suit again. When they looked up Black's and Cricket's stupid assess were sleep, laying on their shoulders standing up. The deadweight of the two men was about to take them down to the floor.

Angel looked at her daughter and said, "You know what time it is?"

She told Angel, "I have mind."

Before Angel could turn her head, Baby Girl grabbed cricket by his neck and snapped it. His body was as limp as a dish rag; he was dead. Angel left Black lying on the floor. She took her piano wire, wrapped it around his neck, and started pulling, but Black wasn't giving in as quickly as Cricket. He was fighting Angel. Baby Girl snuck up behind Black with her switchblade and cut his throat from ear to ear; he slid down from Angel's leg to the floor; he too was now dead.

Angel and Baby Girl packed their shit, checked out the hotel, and headed back to California. They made sure they wiped their fingerprints off everything in that room, including the doorknob on their way out of the room. Angel and Baby Girl made it home just in time to have an envelope delivered to Angel's house. She had another assignment that she had to go on the next morning, so she took the envelope opened it to see who her next target was and she said, *Damn, I thought that I was done with Chicago,* but the Columbians had put a hit out on Mrs. Helen, her dead sister Isabella's mother.

Mrs. Helen was the Columbians connection to the family services she was helping them get some of their people placed in the United States, helping them get passports and keeping immigration from finding out that they were sending people through the system under assumed names.

Helen made it up in her mind that she was tired of taking chances with helping the Columbians. She almost got busted twice on her job, plus they weren't paying her enough to lose her job of twelve years. What Mrs. Helen didn't know was her demise was being recorded and was going to see her daughter Isabella sooner than she thought because Angel was on her way back to Chicago, ready to put Mrs. Helen out of her misery. When Angel drove to Chicago, she went straight to Mrs. Helen's house. She knew she stayed in the same house because she went by her house when she got out of jail, but Angel didn't have it in her soul to apologize to Mrs. Helen about the death of her daughter. She wanted Mrs. Helen to pay for sleeping with her father Cane while he was still married to her mother.

Angel knew in her heart that she was going to kill Helen quickly because she didn't want to waste no more of her time in Chicago right now until it was time to for her come back to resume her position. Angel still owned a lot of property in Chicago, and she wanted to keep everything she owned right there up under her dummy cooperation. Angel broke out Helen's back door window and waited inside for Mrs. Helen to come home. When Mrs. Helen opened her front door and headed straight for her recliner. She would do that every day she came home because her feet would be hurting so bad.

When Mrs. Helen sat down, she let her head fall back against the back of her recliner and closed her eyes and took a deep breath. When she opened her eyes, again it was too late, Angel had an existing cord wrapped around her neck so tight until her eyeballs damn near bulged out her head. Mrs. Helen didn't think that would be the last breath that she took. Mrs. Helen was sitting in her favorite recliner dead as a doorknob. Angel left Mrs. Helen's house through the back door. She jumped on the highway and headed back to California with another job completed.

Chapter Twenty-Six
Angel s Car Accident

A NGEL WAS ON her way back from Chicago when she started feeling dizzy. She tried to keep her eyes focused on the road. It was icy on the highway, and she couldn't pull over because the highway was crowded with people getting off work. Angel tried to swerve her car to the right shoulder on the highway when she was struck by a big truck. Her car got bent up like a Pepsi can. Angel was knocked unconscious. When the ambulance got to the scene of the accident, Angel was lying on the pavement. The man that was driving the truck pulled her out of the car right before it exploded.

Angel was in the hospital for five days, still unconscious. Baby Girl started getting worried because she kept calling Angel's phone and it kept going to her voice mail. Baby Girl called Ramon to let him know that Angel had been missing for five days, and she was worried that something happened to her mother. Ramon told Baby Girl not to worry, he was on his way and that he would be there before dark.

Ramon was at Angel's house as promised. He looked at Baby Girl. She was looking so pale. She hadn't slept in five days. He asked her, "Why didn't you call me days ago?"

She just started crying, "Because I didn't want to throw up any red flags. I was hoping my mother would have called me by now. Something is wrong. I can feel it."

Ramon told Baby Girl, "Calm down. I am going to check the hospitals first to see if they have any Jane Does."

He called three hospitals before he found Angel. She had been admitted in Mercy Hospital outside of the Chicago area under Jane Doe.

She was still unconscious when Ramon and Baby Girl made it up to the hospital. Baby Girl looked at her mother and started crying all over again because Angel didn't look like herself. Her face was swollen like a beach ball. Ramon gave the nurse at the hospital Angel's information so they would know who she was. He wanted her to have round-the-clock care from every staff no matter what the cost was.

Ramon and Baby Girl stayed at the hospital with Angel the whole time. She didn't even know they were there, but they didn't care because they weren't leaving her side. Five days later, Angel was still unconscious. The doctor came in every day to check Angel's vitals.

Ramon and Baby Girl were sitting in a chair in Angel's room sleep when she woke up. She could hardly talk; her mouth was so dry. Angel called Baby Girl's name. She heard her mother coughing. She jumped up and ran over to Angel's bedside. She started hugging and kissing her. She said, "Mommy, I thought you weren't going to ever wake up. I've been praying that you wake up."

Angel looked at Baby Girl like she was crazy because Angel still hadn't realized that she was in the hospital until she saw Ramon standing beside her bed. When Ramon bent down to kiss Angel, that's when it hit her about her being in accident on the highway on her way home.

Angel had a broken pelvis. They had to operate on her to stop the bleeding. She also had a fractured skull. That's why she was still unconscious for so long. Her head was swollen along with her face. She remembered her face hitting the steering wheel. Angel stayed in the hospital for three weeks. She wanted to get back to work, but Ramon told Angel she needed the time off to recuperate. She said fine, but she needed some outpatient therapy as well, so Ramon hired a nurse from the hospital to stay with Angel.

Angel went home three days later, and Ramon stayed with Angel until she got better. He lavished Angel the whole time he was there. He and Baby Girl waited on Angel's hand and foot. She got spoiled the whole time. Angel got herself back on track in no time. She was ready to get back on assignments, but Ramon wanted her to be healed all the way before she went back to work. To make sure she was healing properly, he took Angel and Baby Girl back to Columbia with him for a while.

Angel and Baby Girl had been in Columbia for three weeks. Ramon knew Angel had healed because they were having sex like rabbits. Angel told Baby Girl it was time for them to go back home.

Baby Girl said, "Are you sure? Because I'm having so much fun."

"Here," Angel said, "it's time, Baby Girl. We have jobs, remember?"

She said, "Yes."

Ramon flew them back home that night.

Angel and Baby Girl made it home that night. Angel was waiting on some college letters she had filled out for Baby Girl to go to college. She received three acceptance letters from three colleges that she wanted her daughter to attend. Baby Girl wanted to go to Spelman. She got accepted letter, and she was leaving to go Spelman in two weeks.

Gloria really didn't want to leave her mother, Angel, behind. She knew they both were trained assassins but that didn't keep her from worrying about the safety of her mother. Angel had her mind made up for Baby Girl to get some more education under her belt. It was in parable that she had more than just a high school diploma. Gloria a.k.a. Baby Girl was going to Spelman to get a degree to be a prosecuting attorney. Angel asked Baby Girl, "Are you sure that's what you want a degree in knowing? We are hired assassins."

Baby Girl said, "Yes, I'm sure, Mother, because we might need someone from the inside to help us get out of a messy situation one day."

Angel wanted Baby Girl to get a license in real estate because they had a lot of property on hold under a dummy corporation, but Angel had a plan that she could go get her a real estate license under an assumed name while Baby Girl was away at Spelman. Angel and Baby Girl went shopping to get Baby Girl her school supplies and other things she needed for her dorm room. They were out most of the day. When they returned home, it was another envelope slid under Angel's front door.

Angel didn't want Baby Girl to see the envelope because she wanted her attention to be on going to college, but before Angel could been down and pick the envelope up, Baby Girl snatched it up from off the floor. Before Angel could even bend down, Baby Girl ripped the envelope open to see who their next target was going to be; it was two African brothers named Barras and Baas.

Angel told her daughter that she was going to go solo on this assignment because she was leaving for college in two weeks, and there were no exceptions.

Baby Girl said, "Come on, Mom, one more for the road."

Angel said, "No, and I mean no, Baby Girl."

Baby Girl had the taste of blood on her hands. She liked the rush that it gave her. It made her feel powerful and unstoppable. Angel looked Baby Girl in the eyes, and she could see the killer instinct in her daughter's eyes. She was more than capable to be an assassin.

That night, Angel got the envelope to look over the details of these two African brothers; she wanted to know their story. The two brothers were running the drug trafficking spot in Cleveland, Ohio. They were so busy dressing themselves and getting high off the product that they didn't consider the consequences behind messing up the Columbians' money.

Angel had the details of where the two brothers hung out. She also had the address to their loft on the South Side of Cleveland. The two brothers had opened up a brothel named Queen Bees. They engaged in sexual activities, prostitutes, and orgies; they had prostitutes from all over coming to join in the sexual activities the brothers had going on in their brothel.

Angel said, *These fools made a big mistake going up against the Columbians and to open up a brothel with female prostitution will be my way in, to get close to them fools.* Angel went to Victoria's Secret to pick her up some nice and nasty lingerie she wanted to have the brothers' minds to be completely fucked up.

Angel had a week to get her gear packed up to go to Cleveland. She wanted to see her Baby Girl off to college first, but time wasn't on her side. She would have to go to Cleveland, hit her targets first, and then go to Spelman to make sure her Baby Girl was comfortable in her new surroundings.

Angel was getting her artillery together to take to Cleveland with her when it hit her about taking her Baby Girl to the car lot to get her a new vehicle. Baby Girl didn't have a clue that her mother was going to buy her the car of her dreams. She always wanted a baby blue 2011 convertible Mustang. While they were at the car lot, Angel called ahead to the Hilton Garden Inn in Cleveland to get a reservation for four days.

Angel made Baby Girl so happy to be driving off the car lot with a spanking brand-new convertible straight off the showroom floor. She was as ecstatic. Angel had breakfast with her daughter the next morning before she headed out to Cleveland. Baby Girl kissed her mother and told Angel to have a safe trip, and Angel left going to Cleveland.

Gloria a.k.a. Baby Girl had made plans of her own. She checked into Spelman, got her assignments, and did the same thing her mother did. She called the hotel and made reservations at the same hotel, but on a different floor so she wouldn't get spotted by her mother. She was going to watch her back rather. She wanted her to or not that's what she was trained to do. Baby Girl saw the details of the two brothers when Angel went to bed that night. She knew what her mother was up against, and she wasn't going to let her do it alone.

Angel checked in to the Hilton that morning and rented a Chrysler 300; it came equipped with a GPS. That was one thing she didn't have to order with her rental. She found the brothel in record time. All she had to do now is go in and make herself known. She wanted the brothers to see what she was working with so they could be competing with each other for her attention because the other females in their brothel had nothing on Angel—she knew it and so did they.

Glow was outside the brothel watching the front. She rented her a black Honda Accord. She didn't want to look suspicious. She was going to let her mother know she was there adventitiously, but it would have to wait until later. Later that night, Angel put on a show. She walked in Queen Bees wrapped in a black fur coat with nothing on up under it but a red bra set with red thigh-high stockings with red garters. She had six-inch red pumps on as well.

Glow sat across the street when she saw her mother go into the brothel. She knew something was about to go down. Glow was on high alert; she knew her mother all too well. Glow said to herself, *I need a disguise.* She goggled a store where she could alter her appearance. She needed a wig and some contacts as well. She wanted to make herself look older.

Angel was in the brothel sitting at the bar having an apple martini when Barras came over to her to introduce himself; his accent threw Angel off. She thought that he sounded country as hell to her. She tried really hard not to laugh in his face. Angel looked up in Barras face and said, "Oh, I'm sorry. My name is Candy."

He told Angel, "Of course, your name is Candy because you look as sweet as hell."

Angel responded to Barras comment with, "Is that right?"

He said, "That is right. How about you come over to my place and have some more apple martinis with me?"

Angel agreed to go to Barras's place with him. She wanted to get to know the layout of their loft anyway, so she said to herself, *Typical, man, they always thinking with their little heads. Their dicks are always going to be their downfall because it wants what it wants and when it wants it.*

Angel said, "Oh, well," she told Barras, "let's roll out."

He got up from the bar stool, grabbed Angel's hand, and they left the brothel to go to Barras's loft.

Baby Girl had just pulled back up to the brothel when she saw her mother coming out the door with Barras. He was grinning like someone had given him a free pass to a baseball game. Angel didn't know that the brothers knew the Columbians better than she did. They saw her coming a mile away while she was sitting in the brothel getting her drink on. The brothers were planning to kidnap and kill Angel.

Barras said to himself, *The kidnapping part would be easy if she comes with me willingly.* When he saw that Angel was going with him on her own free will, he knew she was really up to something. While Barras and Angel were on their way to the loft, Barras's brother Baas was already planted at the loft waiting on him and Angel to arrive. Angel had two snug nose thirty-eights sowed inside her fur coat. They would never find her hidden compartment inside her fur coat.

Barras was to get Angel to their loft and feed her martinis lace with cocaine.

Angel asked to use the bathroom as soon as she walked in the front door. Barras said, "Sure, the bathroom is down the hall to your right."

As soon as Angel shut the bathroom door, Baas came out of the den holding a pair of handcuffs. He told his brother, "Soon as that bitch open the bathroom door, you punch her in her face hard enough to knock her out, all right."

Barras said, "I got this. Go back into the den. I will bring her back there once I knock her out."

Baas said okay and disappeared back down the hall.

Angel opened the bathroom door to come out. When she stepped out the door, Barras hit her so hard in her face he broke her nose. Angel went down to the floor so fast she didn't even remember passing out. When she came to, she was handcuffed to Barras's bed. The brothers had planned on raping Angel first before they killed her.

Baas wanted to take his turn raping Angel first. She was his kind of woman he knew; she was a redbone woman. He liked his women light and bright. It was something about a light-skinned woman that made his dick get hard-on.

Barras was angry with his brother because he felt that he was the one who got Angel to come willing with him, so he should have had first go at her. Baas crawled up on Angel's body like he was a python in rear form ready to attack. He started licking all over Angel's body. When his tongue made it to Angel's honey pot, he dipped his tongue so deep in Angel's honey pot until she let out a loud sound of pleasure. He wasn't expecting that. That made him lick even faster because she turned him on like a fire hose on a fire truck.

Barras was getting pissed looking at his brother giving Angel satisfaction. He wanted to be the one to set fire to Angel's honey pot. Barras grabbed his brother off Angel and said, "That's enough. It's my turn."

Barras had gotten a hard-on standing there watching his brother doing Angel. He got on top of Angel and pulled his penis out and drove it hard into Angel's honey pot. His brother said, "Hurry up and bust your nut because I want some of that fat ass she got."

Barras was finished busting his nut in Angel's, so he rested on the side of the bed watching his brother screw Angel in the ass. Angel was so messed up from the cocaine they put in her drink at the brothel that she was actually enjoying what the two brothers were doing to her sexually.

She didn't know what they had plan next for her. They had intentions on beating Angel to death with their bare hands. What they didn't know was that they were about to get hit with the element of surprise. Angel's Baby Girl was coming in through their front door, loaded and locked.

Gloria a.k.a. Angel's Baby Girl kicked the brothers door off the hinges. She came in furious. She knew something was wrong. Her mother was never on a set no longer than an hour. She had been inside the brothers loft for over an hour and half, which sent a bad signal alert to Baby Girl's brain. She had two pearl-handled forty-fives with silencers on them. When the brothers heard their door come down, they didn't grab their weapons because they thought it was Johnny law coming to arrest them.

Barras was the first to run in the living room with his hand up in the air. He was going to surrender without a fight. His brother was right behind him, which they found out was a big mistake. Baby Girl was hitting them all over their bodies with her forty-fives. They were spitting out bullets like a MAC-10. Both brothers dropped to the floor like a pincushion.

Baby Girl was calling out Angel's name, but she couldn't answer her because Baas had covered her up, put duct tape on her mouth to make sure she wouldn't scream. When Baby Girl opened the door to the bedroom, she saw a blanket on the bed with blood on it. She was scared because she didn't want to see her mother dead under that blanket.

When Baby Girl moved the blanket, her mother was bloody from head to toe, but at least she was alive. She had been raped, plus her nose was broken. Baby Girl was so angry she put her mother's coat on her and helped her out the house. Once she put Angel in the car, she went back in the brothers' loft and emptied her guns in both their faces.

Gloria went back to the Hilton, checked her and her mother out, and took the rental car back to enterprise. She then proceeded in taking her mother home to California. Angel was so out of it she didn't even recognize her own daughter. Baby Girl stopped at a hospital on the way back to California as her mother needed medical assistance immediately.

Angel's nose was badly broken. It had to be set back in place. She had been badly raped by both brothers and drugged with cocaine. Baby Girl didn't want them to check her mother for the rape, but she did want them to do something about her nose because Angel could hardly breathe.

Baby Girl didn't want to send up no red flags about her mother being raped. She told the hospital that Angel was her sister and they were out at a club and got jumped by a gang of women. The doctor that was examining Angel was checking out Baby Girl, so if she said the earth was going to blow up, he would have believed her. Dr. Mitchell told Baby Girl to leave the room while he and his nurse examined Angel. She said, "Okay, I'll be right outside the door."

When Dr. Mitchell got through examining Angel, he asked Baby Girl to step back in the room. He said, "I know your sister has been raped, and she has cocaine in her system. You know I have to report my findings to the authorities."

Baby Girl broke down crying telling the doctor to please don't report what he found that she and Angel would be leaving town as soon as he told her she was free to go. Dr. Mitchell told Baby Girl if she had dinner with him and explained what really happened, he may think about not calling the authorities. Baby Girl had dinner with the doctor. She told him that Angel had a boyfriend in town that beat and raped her and that they weren't supposed to be in Cleveland at all.

Dr. Mitchell understood what Baby Girl was saying, and he gave Angel a clean bill of health. The next day, she was released to go home with the stipulation of Baby Girl keeping in contact with him on Angel's condition. She said fine, Angel and Baby Girl hit the highway going back to California.

Angel started to heal nicely. She healed well enough for Baby Girl to go back to college. She left a week later and headed back to Spelman. Angel couldn't even get mad at her daughter for following her to Cleveland. She privately saved her life because if she hadn't secretly followed Angel, she would have never known what happened to her mother. Baby girl went off to college, and Angel missed her dearly. They talked every day on the phone.

Baby Girl even told Angel she met a guy name Raymond. She told Angel he was a cutie, and that he went to another college not far from Spelman, where he majored in criminal justice. Angel let Baby Girl know to be careful while she was away from home to look at everyone differently. "Don't trust anyone."

Baby Girl said, "Yes, Mother, I will be careful. I love you. I will call you next week."

They said good-bye to each other and hung up.

Chapter Twenty-Seven
Angel Moving to Columbia

UNCLE LEO MADE a call to Angel with a good proposition. He wanted Angel to move to Columbia. He had a high-priced escort service he wanted her to run. Angel was a beautiful, classy, and rich woman. She stood out from the crowd of women that was in the escort service. Uncle Leo put Angel in a class all by herself. When Angel answered the phone, she knew it was Uncle Leo. She never had the pleasure of talking on the phone with him. He would always send her envelopes with details, but for him to call her personally, she knew it was personal.

Angel answered, "Hello, Uncle Leo, so why do I have the honor in talking to my favorite?"

Uncle Leo said, "I have a proposition that you cannot refuse."

Angel said, "You do. Okay, let's hear it if it's good. I might not. It depends on what it is."

When Uncle Leo ran the business down to Angel, she was more than happy to take him up on his offer. She would have more money, plus she still would have to go out on assignments once a month. Angel agreed to move to Columbia at the end of the month. Uncle Leo had his moving crew set in position to go to California to move Angel to Columbia.

Angel had everything put in motion to move to Columbia. She wanted to tell Baby Girl personally, so she drove down to Spelman to surprise her daughter, only to be in for a surprise of her own Baby Girl forgot to mention to her mother that she got kicked out of Spelman for selling drugs on campus. Angel had a GPS tracking device put on her daughter's phone before she left home to go to Spelman, but she had totally forgotten until it hit her when she was at Spelman standing there looking lost because Baby Girl had been kicked out of Spelman for two weeks. They talked every day on the phone and she didn't even mention it not once to her mother, so Angel was beyond pissed. She was furious.

Angel turned on the tracking device, and it led her straight to Raymond's dorm room. She couldn't believe what she was looking at her. Baby Girl was sitting there sucking on a glass crack pipe. Angel was trying to figure out what the hell happened in three weeks' time. She grabbed Baby Girl and took her the hell up out of there. She was going to put her daughter in rehab because she had gotten so thin, looked like Baby Girl hadn't took a bath in weeks. Angel really wanted to see this Raymond character because he had strung her daughter out on crack cocaine. He was a dead man whenever Angel caught up with him; it so happened he was out on a drug run when Angel popped up on them.

Baby Girl lied the whole time when she told Angel about him. He was a drug lord. She didn't want Angel to know the truth about Raymond. Angel thought to herself, *I would have felt better if she told me he was a doctor or he was a street pharmacy.*

Angel wasn't too mad at her daughter. She took Baby Girl straight to rehab with restrictions: no visitors, just her. She wanted her to kick her drug habit alone. Without this Raymond person being around, she didn't want her daughter to have no parts of this man. Angel went home and packed her things for the movers to come move her to Columbia. She had her things moved to Columbia, and she went back to stay at the rehab with Baby Girl.

Angel had an epiphany. She thought it would be in her Baby Girl's best interest to take Mr. Raymond off the map. He was really a thorn in Angel's side. She didn't want her daughter traveling in the same circles with him. Baby Girl was a true soldier. She was never a follower.

The rehab had Baby Girl on twenty-four-hour suicide watch. She tried to take her life twice. Angel knew what was bothering her daughter. She had blood all over her hands. Maybe she taught her too early or maybe she just can't handle taking life from another human being. Whatever the cause, Angel was determined to help her daughter out of this situation and get her back on track. But first, she was going to take care of the idiot who sent her Baby Girl to rehab in the first place.

Angel went back to Spelman in Atlanta, Georgia. She wanted to have a sit down with the dean. One thing Angel knew was money talk and bullshit walked. Spelman was a very prestigious and highly selective school for women, and Angel wanted Baby Girl back where she belonged. Angel talked to the dean for hours. When she got done talking with the dean, her Baby Girl was accepted back with no problems.

Angel said a prayer. She said to herself, *I of all people praying but this is for my daughter, not for me. I just need your help, Lord, in watching over my daughter.* After Angel left the dean's office, she made a detour to find this Raymond guy. He had to pay the piper for getting her daughter hooked on crack.

Angel went back to his dorm room where he supposed to be staying. When she pulled up, he ran up to her car like she was a junkie. When he did that, Angel shot Raymond twice in the head. It wasn't a wittiness in sight; she got away real smooth. Baby Girl got out the rehab two months later, and Angel drove her back to Spelman. She explained to Baby Girl that they would be staying in Columbia for a while. Baby Girl was happy that they would be staying in Columbia. She loved it there, especially loved Uncle Leo Sanchez. The Columbian mafia family loved Angel and her daughter.

Angel moved into the villa that Uncle Leo purchased for her. He had it furnished. She was set up in her villa like a Columbian princess. She had set up her computers, opened up her Facebook, Twitter, and e-mail accounts. She was going to run the escort service like a legal business. She had at least twenty exotic women working under her thumb. She felt like a Columbian madam. That's actually what she was. She was an assassin twice a month and a madam the rest of the year. Angel's plate was definitely full.

Chapter Twenty-Eight
Angel s Columbian Madam

ANGEL SETTLED INTO her new villa. She even changed the name Uncle Leo had put on the villa he wants her to run. He called it a Slice of Life. Angel didn't like the name; she asked Uncle Leo if she could change the name to make their clientele want to come visit their establishment. He told Angel, "I want you to do whatever you think will make it popular." Angel had the right name for it. She called their establishment Sexy Ladies.

Angel and Ramon got real close when she moved to Columbia. They spent a lot of time together; she was his little princess. They went on dates. He even took Angel on a canoe picnic. Angel and Ramon had sex on a regular basis. They got so toasted one night they had unprotected sex. She was positive she wouldn't get pregnant. She thought until about two months later Angel started to pick up weight in her hips and breast.

Uncle Leo gave a dinner party to welcome Angel to Columbia. She tried on some of her clothes, but she couldn't fit into nothing. She said to herself, *This isn't right. I could wear this outfit two months ago.* The thought hit Angel she remembered the night she and Ramon had sex without a condom. She said, *Shit! My ass might be pregnant.* Angel went into town to see a doctor. She wanted to see if she was pregnant because she was still having her period, but her body felt different this time.

Angel went to into the doctor's office for visit. She had to sit and wait for a while because she didn't have an appointment. When the nurse called Angel's name, she got up and went in the room where the nurse took her vital signs. She then gave Angel a cup to put some urine in so it could get sent to the lab before the doctor came in to examine her. The nurse told Angel to get undressed from her waist down so the doctor could examine her. She also told Angel the doctor would be in to see her shortly.

Angel was sitting there waiting for the doctor to come in. She was so deep in thought she didn't even hear the doctor knock on the door before he entered the room.

He asked Angel, "Why do you want to see me today and what are your concerns?"

She told the doctor, "I have been gaining weight and feel sleepy all the time, and I haven't missed my period, but my body feels different."

The doctor told Angel to lay back and scoot down to the end of the table so he could examine her.

When Angel did what the doctor told her to do, the nurse came back in the room with Angel's urine test results. Angel was indeed pregnant. When the doctor finished his examination, he told Angel why her body felt so different. He told Angel she has a disorder they call preeclampsia. It's a disorder that occurs during pregnancy and that the postpartum period which affects both the mother and unborn baby.

Dr. Bishop went on to explain a little more about preeclampsia so Angel could understand the disorder more clearly. He told Angel that the symptoms, often in women who have preeclampsia, they do not feel sick, but the symptoms of preeclampsia included swelling of the hands and face and eyes, plus she can have sudden weight gain. The condition also included pregnancy hypertension.

Angel asked the doctor, "What is the treatment for preeclampsia?"

He told Angel, "There are a lot of different treatments for the condition." He also told Angel, "It's a high risk pregnancy."

Angel had a lot to think about when she left the doctor's office. She really wasn't ready to tell Ramon about what she just went through. She just wanted to marinate on the situation for a little while before she told him. Angel made it back to the villa. She started back to work; she didn't act like nothing was going on with her. She was hired by Uncle Leo to do a job and that's what she was doing: her job.

One Friday morning, Angel got the girls up for a doctor's appointment. That's one thing for sure she made very clear to the women that they had to take test to make sure no one had any venereal diseases. She had the doctor to give her all the girls' test results to her. She made sure each and every one of them had a supply of condoms. It was one bad apple in the whole bunch of women; her name was Teri. She didn't like Angel; she thought that Angel was a little young to be the madam of the establishment.

Teri wanted to talk to Uncle Leo about Angel. She didn't want no child telling her what to do. She felt like she was old enough to be Angel's mother. Teri went up to the villa to confront Uncle Leo about how she felt about how Angel ran things.

Uncle Leo told Teri, "If you don't like what is going on, you can leave, but you cannot take nothing with you."

Teri was angry because she felt that she was the one bringing in the most money she deserved to keep whatever she had.

Uncle Leo told Teri, "You better not start any trouble because if you do, I will hang you from a tree buck naked so the whole village could see you for the whore you really are."

Angel knew Teri was going to be trouble because before Uncle Leo called her to run the place, Teri was running it down to the ground. She was stealing money, letting the girls do what they wanted as long as the money came back to her. The only reason Uncle Leo kept her around because he promised her father before he killed him that Teri would always be taken care of and she would never whine up on the street.

Angel took the women shopping to get some proper, well-needed clothing. They dressed like homeless hookers. She wanted the women to be appropriate to look the part of being lady callers of the night, not like they came from a hoe stroll on the streets of Chicago. They were all beautiful women; she wanted to make them look high-class, elegant, and glamorous women that's who they were. She even did all of their makeup. When Angel got finished with her makeover on all the women, Uncle Leo could hardly contain himself.

Teri was still making trouble. She started trying to turn the other women against Angel. She told the women that they were the ones doing all the fucking, and Angel was reaping the benefits. Teri also told the women that Angel was fucking Uncle Leo: "How do you think she got the job to be the madam? She came all the way from California to stay down here, I don't think so. That bitch is Leo's personal assassin. Now she done moved here to Columbia to take over as madam. That's some bullshit, and we all know that."

Angel had a few of the girls that she was close to. One for sure she was close enough with that she got gossip from when Teri kept sticking her foot in her mouth. Angel decided it was time to call Teri in her office so she could get whatever her problem was with her off her chest. Angel was hoping she didn't have to kick Teri's ass to get her point across, but she wasn't worried. She said to herself, *Let the chips fall where they may because this shit ends today.*

Teri strutted in Angel's office with an attitude she was ready for war. Little did she know she was dealing with the right one because Angel wanted to stomp a hole in Teri's ass just on general principle. Angel asked Teri to have a seat, but she declined. Angel said, "All right, whatever I called you in here today because I heard you didn't like the way I was running things."

Before Angel could say another word, Teri said, "I don't like the way you came all the way from California with your want to be pretty ass trying to run things different from the way I was running them."

Angel looked at Teri and said, "Oh, you angry because I stopped your little side hustle."

Teri said, "Look here, bitch, you didn't stop shit. Leo's fucking your little stank ass. That's why he chose you to replace me because he wasn't getting no more free pussy."

Angel made it clear to Teri saying, "If you call me a bitch just one more time, they would be zipping your ass up in a plastic bag."

Teri started balling her fist up real tight. She told Angel, "if you feel threatened by me jump or do your heart pump Kool-Aid bitch."

Teri knew deep down she didn't have a chance with Angel. She knew just like everyone else in Columbia that Angel was a killer for hire why she was trying to go up against her was beyond Angel. When Teri spit bitch out her mouth again, Angel jumped across her desk and hit Teri so hard in her jaw she broke it on impact. Teri tried to grab Angel's long ponytail to pull her hair. Angel said, "No, bitch, you asked for an ass whipping, and I'm the right bitch to give you what you asked for."

Angel and Teri were going at so hard one of the women in the house ran up to the villa to get Uncle Leo and Ramon. They stood there for a minute because they haven't seen two women fight in a long time, plus Angel had yet to tell them she was pregnant. When Ramon and Leo pulled them apart, Teri looked like she had been in a boxing ring with Sugar Ray Leonard for two rounds. She was torn up; both her eyes were black.

Uncle Leo told Teri, "I warned you what was going to happen if you started any trouble."

He grabbed Teri by her hair and snatched her clothes off, and Ramon hung her outside in the tree. He took a bullwhip and beat Teri until she passed out. Teri hung in that tree for three days before Leo took her down. She went back to work in Sexy Ladies with Angel without another word. She acted like her tongue had been cut out her mouth. She didn't speak to anyone for a month; her body was sore the whole time.

Chapter Twenty-Nine
Angel and the Columbian Cartel

UNCLE LEO HAD some problems with the Columbian cartel. They were about to go to war over Uncle Leo's territory. They had begun to overstep their bounds. The Columbian cartel was kicking in the wrong doors. They were sending threatening messages to the Columbian mafia that they were taking over the West Side of Columbia. Uncle Leo and his crew had to move out or get push out. It was a lot of money to be made on the West Side, and they made it known that everybody on that set was getting shut down.

Uncle Leo wasn't about to let it go down like that. He prepared all his soldiers for war. He even had his secret weapon on standby. Angel was geared up she had weapons for mass destruction. She was just waiting for Uncle Joe, who is Uncle Leo's eldest brother, to give her the green light. Angel was about to turn in for the night when Uncle Joe called for her to come up to their villa. She put on her ninja suit and headed out the door.

Uncle Joe wanted Angel to go over on the West Side of Columbia to set up C4 everywhere. He wanted the whole West Side blown off the map. Uncle Joe even had part of the military paid in full to kill everybody in the Columbian cartel. The cartel had more pull than Uncle Joe thought. They heard about how they get down and dirt, plus the cartel had an inside connection. Teri was straddling both sides of the fence. She was getting back at them for what Uncle Leo did to her, plus she wanted Angel's ass gone.

Uncle Leo said somebody around their camp been trading secrets. He said, "The motherfuckers knew too much, and if I find out who it is, they're going to die a slow and agonizing death. I want everyone to take a lie detector test right now. Wake everybody up. I'm not going to rest until I find out who in my camp had the nerve to trade secrets with my fucking enemies."

Angel thought to herself, That bitch Teri been awful quite around here. I'll bet a million dollars that she's the culprit, and if she is, I feel sorry for the bitch, because what Uncle Joe planning on doing to the trader is like pulling teeth with wire pliers.

Everyone was up in the compound was taking lie detector test, including Angel. That's when they found out she was pregnant because she still hadn't told anyone until that night.

Everyone passed the lie detector test but Teri. Uncle Joe was pissed. He told everyone they could go back to their villas. He told Teri, "You can stay. I have business to straighten out with you."

Before Teri could say another word to defend herself, Uncle Joe said, "Bitch, don't you utter a word. The only sound I'm going to hear from you is screaming. You made your bed, and you damn sure going to lay in it. I knew you were going to be trouble the day my brother killed your father, but he made a promise to your father to take care of you. Now you will be dancing with your father in hell."

Uncle Joe, Uncle Leo, and Ramon took Teri to the gun house. They strung her up to a high beam they had in the ceiling. She was screaming and crying real loud. Uncle Joe told Teri, "You can scream as long as you want for now because that's the last sound we're ever going to hear coming out of your mouth."

Uncle Joe took a blow torch and burned all of Teri's skin off her body. When he was through with burning Teri alive, he took some alcohol and dashed it all over her burned skin you could smell Teri's flesh burning like she was getting roasted like a side of beef.

Everyone in their villas could hear Teri screaming. Then all of a sudden, the screaming stopped. It was over. The girls knew that Teri would eventually write a check her ass couldn't cash. Angel was glad Teri wasn't around to start any more trouble; truth be told, she was going to bust a couple of caps in Teri's ass herself.

Angel put the C4 around the Columbian cartel's compound like she was told to do. She had all the detonators all ready to go when she was ready to blow their compound up. Wasn't anyone getting too much sleep that night after the Columbian mafia killed Teri that night. It was very quiet until they heard a big boom. It was bombs being set off all over the compound. The Columbian cartel had snuck in under the radar. They were blowing up Uncle Leo's compound. They had people running outside with their bodies blazing with fire. Angel and Ramon made it underground to their safe house. Everyone else, including his uncles and the call girls were all dead; nothing was left.

Angel and Ramon had to find a way to get out of Columbia without getting caught. Their lives were in danger. The cartel was still hot on their trail until Angel remembered that she had their camp set up to blow up as well. She set off her detonators and the compound blew up as well. But she didn't get a chance to kill all of their people. Mr. Sanchez, the head of the cartel, got trapped in his car. It blew up as soon as his driver tried to turn the ignition. His son was being held by one of his soldiers. He was trying to break away from him to save his father, but it was too late. Mr. Sanchez's car was up in the air like it was being carried away by twister.

Marcos, Mr. Sanchez's son, wanted heads for his father's death. He knew who was responsible because Teri had filled him in on Angel the Columbian assassin for the Columbian mafia. He knew all too well who she was. He even had pictures of Angel. He knew her daughter Gloria went to Spelman. That made Marcos think he was going to the states to find Angel's daughter to bring Angel out of hiding. Marcos was going to either kill Angel or her daughter, but he was so angry he said to himself, *They both must die. I've lost everything. My whole family is dead because of that bitch Angel. She has to pay with her life and the life of her child.*

Angel and Ramon escaped from Columbia. They got passed the Columbian police, snuck on to Ramon's helicopter, and flew back to California, where they stayed in a hotel under assumed names. They had to find an apartment because Angel was carrying his firstborn child. He promised Angel that everything would be okay, but they both knew that was a lie as long as Marco was alive. He would be looking for them.

Marco arrived in California. He didn't even know where to begin to look for Angel. He didn't even know what part of California she was staying in, but he did have a postcard from her daughter that she sent her from Spelman while Angel was in Columbia that Teri gave him. He also had a picture of Gloria too. Marco knew if he kidnap Gloria, Angel would come out from under a rock to save her daughter, but what Marco didn't know was Angel's Baby Girl was a hired assassin as well.

Marco arrived in Atlanta, Georgia, the next day by airplane. He rented a car and proceeded to Spelmam. He was so distraught that he didn't even check in to a hotel. Marco wanted Angel to pay with blood. She and Ramon were the cause for all his problems. They took his son and his wife away from him; his son was only two weeks old when Angel blew up their compound. In Marco's mind, he wanted Angel's daughter to meet the same fate that his wife and son met.

Angel got in touch with Gloria a.k.a. Baby Girl at school to let her know about everything that happened. She wanted her daughter to be on the lookout for Marco. She even sent Baby Girl photos of Marco so she would know what he looks like. Baby Girl let her mother know that she had everything under control. She even told Angel that she has all her artillery locked and loaded just in case he shows up.

Angel said, "Be careful, and I will be there to join you in a couple of days."

Angel and Ramon flew to Atlanta, Georgia, to be with Baby Girl even though Angel knew her daughter could handle herself. She just wanted to be there to watch her back.

Marco stayed outside campus watching Baby Girl. She peeped him outside, so she made a mental note of the license plates. She knew what her mother told her was right because everywhere she went that same car would show up, so Baby Girl stayed alert. She knew never to get caught slipping that wasn't in the assassin rule book. Angel made reservations at the Ramada Inn. She didn't want to stay in a high-priced hotel this time; she wanted to stay somewhere Marco would stay. She had planned to follow him when he left Spelman. She and Baby Girl had a trap plan for Marco Sanchez.

Ramon hit the GPS to find a costume store. He wanted them be in disguise; he knew just how to get Marco Sanchez off his square. He wouldn't be looking for them to be disguised. Ramon had him and Angel costumes to be made up like two old people. Baby Girl was going to disguise herself as a drag queen by name Raphael. The three of them were going way out on the limb for this kill; they wanted Marco as bad as he wanted them.

Angel wanted her daughter to lower Marco to a hotel so they could wait in the room for him to enter. Angel knew he wasn't going to follow her daughter voluntarily, so she had to pretty much force his hand. Marco saw Gloria go into the Holiday Inn, but he didn't know what room she disappeared into, so he paid the front desk clerk two hundred dollars to give him the room number and a key. He told the clerk that they were married and it was their anniversary and he wanted to surprise his wife.

The clerk gave Marco the room number and a master key to the room. When Marco made it up to the third floor and spotted room 333, he slid the master key in the door. He heard the shower running, so he just knew he had the upper hand on Gloria. When he stepped in the bathroom with his weapon drawn, he was hit from the back with an ashtray. He was knocked out and tied up to a chair.

When Marco came to, he had a hell of a headache; his head was bleeding badly it was blood dripping down his face. He opened his eyes and saw Angel. He started kicking, trying to get loose. He hated Angel. He wanted to kill her with his bare hands. Ramon had three forty-fives with silencers on them. He gave Baby Girl and Angel one; they all stood back, looked at Marco, and let loose. They all emptied their guns in Marco. Once he dropped his head, they knew it was a done deal and he was never going to be after them again. But what Angel, Ramon, and Baby Girl didn't know was the Columbian cartel was a big operation: Mr. Sanchez's brother named Josh had four sons that will be looking for them with vengeance.

Angel took her Baby Girl back to Spelman. She also let Baby Girl know that she was three months pregnant and she will be having a brother or sister in six months. Baby Girl was jumping for joy. She really wanted to have another sibling that she could pass the training on to as well. Angel and Ramon moved back to California for good. They bought a ranch-style home and decorated the nursery for their new addition to the family.

Angel and Ramon found out a year later that Uncle Joe and Uncle Leo got out of the compound underground as well. They got out through the tunnel under Uncle Joe's bedroom, but they didn't want to contact them until it was safe to do so. The uncles wanted to resurface when the close was clear, and when they put the mafia back together.

Angel took care of her preeclampsia condition, and her last two months of pregnancy, she had to stay in bed on bed rest. Her two months was coming fast she had an ultrasound. She had to take tomorrow she would know when her baby actually was due. While Angel was up showering for her ultrasound appointment, her water broke. She was going to have her baby the day she was to take the ultrasound.

Angel and Ramon rushed to the hospital when she got there. She was in full labor. She was in labor an hour before she had a seven-pound eight-ounce twenty-one-inch baby boy. Ramon was bursting with joy. While Ramon was admiring his new son, Uncle Joe called to let him know that the mafia family was back in control and that they needed him and Angel to come back to Columbia, but Ramon told his uncle that Angel just gave birth to a baby and now wouldn't be a good time. Angel had to at least wait six weeks before she could do anything, but they would be in touch.

Uncle Joe said, "Sure, you guys enjoy your son. I will be in touch. Tell Angel we all love her and congratulations and her job still awaits her."

Angel was waiting to go back to work as a Columbian assassin she just had to get rid of her baby weight. Once she did that, she would be right back on top of her game. Angel has twisted and turned all through her whole life. She can't stop now.

Angel the Columbian assassin—the saga continues!

Acknowledgments

I want to thank everyone who reads my book, and for taking this journey with me. I want to thank my husband (William) for having my back with his help of financial help and support. I also want to thank my three granddaughters (Jasmine, Keiasia and Sharaine) for their support in sending e-mails. I want to thank my two grandsons (Kaylen and Keith). I want to thank all of my family members and friends for being there for me and giving me a listening ear and constructive feedback. Thanks for being my supporters in my journey. I'll try my best not to let anyone down. You guys have a special place in my heart. I also want to thank the publishing company and their staff for helping me in publishing my book.

So much love
Brenda G. Wright

CPSIA information can be obtained at www.ICGtesting.com
Printed in the USA
LVOW07s1119130514

385588LV00001B/104/P